◇ THE VEILED SAGAS ◇

THE WRONG SIDE

To Dad, who has helped me through every step.

TABLE OF CONENTS

◆

Beyond the Veil, through space and time, is a realm undreamt of. A place with the glowing eyes of a sorceress and the quaking wails of titans, with the forgotten oaths of failed warlords and double-edged promises of cyberspace.

Breathe the dead air of the Underground, the stinking heat of Yarldom marshes and the mists of NeoAnglian shores. Lords and ladies live in twenty-first century luxury while backwater peasants die of the pox. In dire circumstances, the Exposed join this world. They come as the missing, the vanished, the forgotten... the nameless.

A realm of monsters and magic, of blades and bullets, where kings and heathens rule.

On the Wrong Side, nothing is right anymore.

These are The Veiled Sagas.

◆

PART 1
EXPOSURE

"Through the Veil, you have entered the Wrong Side.
Nothing is right anymore."

Exposure

Rob stumbled into the diner, feeling half-drunk, dizzy and completely terrified. He hit the counter hard, almost falling off the stool.

He ordered a coffee without looking up, he tried to reason out what had happened. Some kid in a Halloween mask, a damn good one, had tried to jump him in a back lane three blocks from his house. It was dark out. The kid was hidden and waiting. A gargoyle face sprang out into view, with teeth and glowing yellow eyes. *It was just so real.*

Scared the crap outta me.

He just ran. He was a Triathlon champion for three years before he got trapped working late at that *god forsaken* firm. So he ran. He would run home, he'd be safe there.

When he turned the corner, he was in the middle of the park across the highway from his neighbourhood. Benches on his left and pine trees on his right. He tried to phone for help, but his android was dead. He tried to call for help, but couldn't find anyone.

He began to walk in one direction back towards the highway. One direction. One step at a time. He went around a huge oak tree and found himself in the middle of a farmer's field.

When he turned around, he saw the city with its lights, its sprawling suburbs, and towering downtown.

He was lost and the diner was the first thing he saw. The flickering lights, the smell of grease and the three vehicles in the parking lot told him he'd find help.

"Here ya go, sweetie," said a girl's voice.

"Thank you," he looked up and almost spat up his coffee.

The waitress was a gorgeous, almost inhuman in her perfection, as if the light sparkled off her. She was a young girl with green eyes and long chestnut hair pulled into a braid and woven with ribbon.

Her pale ears rose up along the sides of her skull into perfectly delicate points.

"You okay, sweetie?"

♦

Confession

"Bless me father, for I have sinned."

"What is your sin, my child? Speak freely." Father Cornelius recognized Daphne Green's voice. A young woman who worked the lodge with her husband.

The young woman's voice cracked. "I am an adulterer, father. I have laid with another man, not my husband."

Of course, she had. Daphne Green was no saint, not a monster, but a human. A human with human weakness. With the clientele that the lodge attracted, Cornelius was surprised he wasn't hearing about this once a week.

"Tell me what happened, my child. God understands the frailty of human weakness. Tell me, was this of lust or of love?"

"Lust."

"Lust is sinful, but forgivable. We all lust. We are human."

"Then why do I feel so truly awful."

"Guilt is good, guilt is how god reminds us to set ourselves back on the right path."

She coughed, "It's not that, father. This man. A stranger. He had skin as pale as milk, he drove a hearse with tinted windows and wore a shirt that was decades old. Who wears a shirt that old?"

Cornelius laughed. "Men do, my child." *This one is actually getting kind of entertaining.* "Go on."

"This man, he did things like I hadn't even thought a man could do. We did things, and ever since my entire body has felt sick. Sick and disgusted."

"This will pass. Does your heart feel lighter? Certainly the forgiveness of god may lift your spirits."

"Father! I am not talking about guilt. Ever since that night, I have felt different. It hurts to leave the house. I tried to visit my mother's and it felt like I was electrocuted when I walked through the door." She shuffled on the other side of the panel. "It hurt to enter the church. My entire body feels hot, like I'm leaking through every pore."

Dumb girl caught something from this stranger. "This may be beyond spiritual assistance, my child. The good doctors may be able to assist you."

She shuffled, growling, "I don't know if they can help me!" she struck the side of the panel. "I can smell you, father! I can smell your blood. It drums in my ears. Please god, help me!"

♦

Remembrance

"We saved them. We saved them all."

"Yes, and they don't remember that we did."

Stalwart ran his hands through his platinum blonde hair. The subtle point of his ears grazing his wrist. "That was the deal."

His sister nodded. "That was the price we paid for victory."

"You, I and only a few dozen more know what happened that day, ten thousand years ago. Only we will ever know."

His sister grew annoyed. "Gods, will you just get over it!? We made the deal. We win, but our victory won't be remembered. What we did is barely known by half the world."

"Far less than half, don't you kid yourself."

"Enough. Many died that day, and many more will die when they return. For now, the world survives and that's enough for me."

Stalwart's silence was louder than his complaints.

His sister scoffed. "Such a man. When a woman raises a child, it's her duty to carry on in silence. When a man does it, he wants a laurel for every diaper changed.

"I get it, I do. I'm just sad, alright?"

His sister chewed her lip. "Then it's something you'll just have to live with." She left him to sit alone in the hall. A long structure of interwoven saplings. A beautiful wicker room centered on a six thousand year old hearth. Ages of fires had turned the pit black as pitch.

Stalwart hadn't seen the outside world in almost two thousand years. The flight of the Romans from the Isles was the last thing he remembered. The last time men had invaded these realms.

The world had forgotten them entirely.

Stalwart turned over the device in his hands. A smartphone. Belonging to a recently Exposed human from Manchester. All the world's accumulated knowledge in his hand and they still didn't know what he had done to save them, ten thousand years ago.

♦

Noodles

The tiny old woman hunched over a searing hot flattop grill, scrambling bits of chicken, shitake mushrooms, sprouts and onions. The hot sizzle was calming, the only constant in her long life.

Sweat poured down her furrowed brow.

With the toppings cooking she had timed it perfect with the cooking noodles. She strained the delicate ramen under cold water before depositing them into a ceramic bowl.

Her thin arms reached back to ladle thick syrupy sauce over the meat and vegetables. With a flick off her spatula, she slid everything into the bowl. Perfect muscle memory. She had done this more times than she could imagine. Every day since she was allowed by the grill.

With a perfect flourish she placed half a hard-boiled egg at the edge of the bowl.

The customer waited patiently with a friendly smile. His gaze made her nervous. *Those eyes aren't right.*

The woman ladled sweet miso broth over the ramen, rejuvenating everything in the bowl. Lines of steam rose around her.

She turned and placed the bowl on the bar in front of the customer. A tall and ethereally beautiful young man with sunlight coloured hair and diamond-shaped black eyes. His pointed-ears rose up along his head.

He smiled and thanked her. The woman bowed, but before she could begin the long process of cleaning up, the customer coughed. "You wouldn't happen to have a fork would you?"

She frowned when she saw him struggling with using both chopsticks and a spoon.

"You use chopsticks here. Proper etiquette."

He frowned. "I am two hundred years old; I understand etiquette. I don't understand these."

The old woman crossed her arms, "I'm eighty-three and I've been making this meal since I could stand. Respect the tradition."

The elf's eyes went wide. Stunned that the old mortal creature who had such passion and confidence. He struggled for his next words…

She sighed, annoyed. "I'll show you."

♦

Moon's Night

Rebecca sat at the edge of camp. Her hands busy with carving a piece of maple into a stallion for Cane and Walda's new cubs. She flicked away the woodchips on to the grass. The evening light drawing closer to darkness. Orang-

11

es and violets of the most exquisite shades dancing through the pine trees.

Her slightly-pointed ears twitched at the nearing foot-steps. The particular vintage of musk told her it was Cartus, the pack's leader.

She glanced back, hopeful, "And?"

Cartus was huge, with long bristling hair along his cheeks and arms. He shrugged, "Too early to tell. Walda is strong, but it's been a hard winter."

Rebecca nodded, the anxiety refusing to let up.

The springtime birds and insects buzzed throughout the forest. The night drawing near.

"Moon's Night. You ready?"

Rebecca put down the toy. "Depends. Will we be monsters or not?"

"You know we can't just keep living off sheep and deer. We need man-flesh in order to sustain ourselves." Cartus paused. "Walda needs it. It will help the cubs."

Rebecca sneered. "If the humans find out what we really are, then every hunter for a hundred miles will be gunning for us."

"I understand that. We have a plan."

Rebecca looked out through the forest. On the other side of the mountain was a town. A tourist town, full of fat men and their families. Land developers, oil tycoons and the rural peasants who bend over for them. Rebecca had every reason to want to strip them down to nothing.

"We will have to be careful. Mass Exposure is dangerous. Stepping into their world to bring them back is very dangerous."

"Don't worry so much." Cartus looked up. "It's time."

Rebecca nodded.

Back at the camp, the pack had gathered. Thirteen members — soon to be fifteen — if they were lucky. They had all stripped themselves of their day-walker clothes. Leaving nothing but bone necklaces, ill-fitting belts and scrap armor.

Cartus dropped his vest just as his eyes turned yellow and the hair criss-crossed on his back. He laughed, letting out a howl announcing the Moon's Night. The pack responded in kind with their murderous chorus.

♦

Medica

Sera Numas leaned against a counter, trying to take the weight off her ankles. She had worked in the Saint Noel Medica for three years now. She had been a nurse on the Right Side. When she was Exposed it had been an easier transition period than most. Franco was certainly easier to live in than most other places on the Wrong Side.

She shifted the weight on her legs. *Two more hours,* she told herself.

"You alright?" asked Basil.

Basil Morekes, the only faun on staff. His brown hair curled around the stubby horns on his forehead. It had taken Sera a month to stop starring at them.

"Just a long day," she replied.

"Things okay at home?"

Sera had started dating again. First time since her Exposure. Since losing another boyfriend... *and my entire world.*

"We're good. He's good," said Sera. "He's sweet. Took me on a carriage ride and then to the park. I felt like a princess."

Basil laughed. "That's like taking a cab ride."

"I know… but it was sweet. Simple. Maybe that's all I need." After years of adjusting to a new world…

A bell rung. They didn't have pagers here. One of their two ambulances was arriving with a critical patient.

Basil and Sera rushed to emergency. The clop of Basil's hooves echoed down the hallways.

From the back of the re-purposed hearse, two medics carried a man in a stretcher. He was restrained, delirious, tears flowing down his face, a sword slash down his front. Just shallow enough that he might survive.

Basil rushed forward to help the attending doctor, Doctor Bennet, who followed the stretcher. "What happened?"

"Bandit raid," said the medic.

Basil and Sera followed along. Sera wasn't paying attention.

The man blinked. He saw Basil and screamed. "What is that?! What the fuck is that?!"

Basil looked at Bennet. Bennet looked at Sera.

Sera was looking at his clothes. They were polyester, cotton, machine made. The fear in his eyes. The confusion. The sheer horror at the sight of the faun.

Sera looked up at Doctor Bennet. "He's been Exposed."

◆

Resort

Edgar Clermont crept through the resort's lounges, a predator searching for prey.

His open collar, cologne, styled hair and wiry arms were only camouflage for his trap. His crimson eyes and pheromone hypnotism would ensure the final snap of the trap. Like a Venus Fly Trap, he would bring the meat closer.

He found one maiden in a blue and gold jumper. A gold chain resting deep in her caramel cleavage. It was certainly warm out.

She looked unhappy.

He swooped in beside her. "Penny for your thoughts?"

She didn't smile immediately. "Hubby abandoned me for the slot machine."

"His loss."

"Vacation has just been a nightmare. Our rooms were still under construction when they gave us the key. Drywall and plaster everywhere. Can you believe that? Who does that?"

He ordered a glass of red wine, a merlot. "Places like this are pits for sucking up money. They don't actually care about you're experience."

"I guess."

That's when she turned to meet his eyes.

All her annoyance and defiance evaporated. The dumb cow-eyed smiled grew across her gorgeous heart-shaped face.

The vampire smiled back.

Easy eating tonight.

♦

Fume

The mercenary entered the den after a damn good job. His wallet full of hard-earned cash. He fell into one of the couches and pulled off his toque and scarf. Winter was coming, and it was going to hit hard. His green eyes fell on the dealer sitting at the bar. A heavy-set man with a face like an abused bulldog.

The dealer's eyes went wide. He ignored his current client and rushed over to the seat opposite of the mercenary.

The mercenary smiled, "How you doing, Poindexter."

"It's Dex, sir. I got your stuff."

The mercenary smiled, he was young, barely into his twenties. Dex already had flecks of silver in his scruff. Sweat leaked down the dealer's neck as he reached into his pocket for an inhaler. Like anything from a pharmacy, the cylinder was shiny chrome but the spout was wrapped with dirty rubbed-shiny masking tape.

With a shaky hand Dex handed the mercenary the inhaler. The mercenary smiled and handed over a bundle of bills.

The dealer looked confused. Usually he tested it before paying.

"You've been reliable, Dex. Thanks."

The dealer nodded and slunk away to the filthy hole he crawled out of.

The mercenary — Marek — was left alone. His headache had only gotten worse since the job. Once the gunfire quieted, the pounded only increased. *Do it, keep me quiet!* Screamed the voice in his head. *It won't work forever! One day you'll have to remember. One day!*

Marek pressed the inhaler to his lips and depressed the button.

He breathed in and a rush of warm sensation rushed through his limbs, all the way to his fingers. His headache vanished, the voice silenced, and he grinned. Instead of smoke, a long tendril of blue flame left his mouth. His tongue felt tingled and tasted of rotten eggs. He could smell the burning chemicals drive up his nose.

The sensation of quiet in his brain was all he needed in this dump yard of a town.

Soon, Marek would move on. On the hunt. For jobs, for money, for Fume.

But mostly, just running away from his past.

♦

Outcasts

Marek and Ana sat around the campfire while everyone else was asleep. Laying in heaps by the fire or curled up in the van. The band of outcasts needed their rest. They had been traveling the Yarldoms for less than a month.

They were trying to stop a war.

A war between backward feuding Yarls. A crew of outcasts trying to manipulate warlords into an uneasy peace.

Marek was fiddling with his handgun. Ana watched him, wrapped in a blanket. He was twenty-two, nearly feral, and viciously intelligent. He'd be handsome if it wasn't for the scar running from his mouth to his ear.

"You're starring again," said Marek, not looking up.

"I'm just wondering where you got that?" said Ana, poking at her cheek.

He shrugged. "I don't remember?"

"You said you weren't Exposed."

"Doesn't mean I remember." He looked up with vivid green eyes. "How much do you remember of your life on the Right Side?"

"Plenty," said Ana. "Just not everything. I know I'm from Winnipeg, somewhere in Transcona, but I couldn't remember the street or how to get there." *Or my mom's name and face...* Exposure took the most important parts from you.

Marek returned to his busy work. The wind whistled through the forests around camp.

"What about your parents?" asked Ana, trying to fill the silence.

Marek put down the gun. Starring intensely at Ana. "You want to share our childhoods? Become friends? Last time I checked if I don't follow your orders I don't get paid. I'll help you, but only so I can get my money."

The snap shut Ana up.

Before Marek returned to his weapon maintenance he said, "Both my parents were Exposed in the eighties as children..."

"From where?"

He refused to say anything more after that.

How the hell are we going to stop this war? We can barely stop fighting each other.

PART 2
THE UNDERGROUND

"Beneath the Rokki Mountains, without sunlight, grew a realm of cities."

Plague

"Mama, listen to me!"

"I'm not going to listen to some human's whore!"

Brynhild stood in the doorway of the hall. The stone walls had been so warm for so long. Now? Brynhild was stunned at how cold they were. "I didn't do anything! It was a kiss!"

"That's how it starts! Those humans just take and take and take. They don't build! They don't forge! They don't mine!"

"What? Like Pa did, before he died in a cave in!?"

"Don't you say a word against your father! By Odin and Frigg, he was a proper dwarf. Dutiful. Kingly."

"With a martyr's complex."

Mama was aghast. She sat at the end of the hall, nalbinding socks. Always socks. "How dare you?"

Brynhild coughed "—How dare I!" she crossed around the hearth. "I'm living my own damn life! He's a nice boy, no honour duels, no blood oaths. Just a nice boy working at the docks. I might even marry him!"

Mama huffed.

"I could do plenty worse trying to find some smiths and the mines for another binge drinking and wife beating bearded Dwerg."

"Don't you use that word here in my home!" Mama was on her feet. The bone needle and yarn scattered on the floor. "Just go, Brynhild! Leave! Go be with your beardless little urchin!"

The pain welled up in Brynhild's chest. She coughed again, hard this time. Her throat felt raw.

Brynhild was angry. She wanted to hurt Mama. Hurt her in the only way a daughter could. Brynhild coughed again. "I will! I don't like the feeling of hair between my thighs anyways!"

Mama fell back into her seat.

Brynhild left, the tears streaming down her cheeks. She was so angry; she didn't notice the blood she coughed into her hand. The year 1919 by Gregorian.

◆

The Underground

It was the first day in six months where Daniel used a day for himself. He should have taken an easy day. A reporter doesn't get weekends. *You're always on call.* He felt it was important to learn more about his new home. The Underground. The metropolis depths of the Rocky Mountains. He looked up, seeing the cavern ceiling bathed in lights from below.

A few RoofSide settlements, as they were called, grew like barnacles between stalactites the size of buildings. Tiny housing blocks carved into the rock or built up with reinforcements.

He sat on double-decker bus. The District number ten painted on its red chassis. The dataslate at the front rail played the news feeds. The date was March 3rd, 2014.

The bus was headed towards the centre of the District. MidTown.

The PillarTowers rose up to the ceiling of the immense cavern. The titanic structures built in endless additions looked like trees with sprawling fungi growing horizontal. Metal and cement build up spread out from the Pillars. Strips and boardwalks in spirals or levels rising all the way up to the roof. Businesses, firms, diners and hundreds of people's livelihoods hugged the side of the Towers. Lights flashed in waves with the thousands of neon signs and passing vehicles.

A holo-projection played wolves climbing across the buildings, leaping and bounding up the structure.

A garden of corporate spires surrounded the PillarTowers. Dozens of buildings reached towards the ceiling. Some dark, some chrome, some white, some gothic, some classical. It was an apocalypse of bad taste and conflicting trends.

A belly dancer the size of a skyscraper gyrated against the side of one spire. Projected onto the side of a hundred Corpfirms.

Daniel spun a pen in my hand, writing down the street names that he couldn't pronounce properly. *Thane Dujhaladin Avenue and Fifth SpikSpekSpite*. It was a new world. It was terrifying.

And Oddly exciting.

He had been Exposed a year ago.

What had been an interview for his small-town paper became an ambush. A monster had brought him to this world. He had been saved. It was all a blur, like shadows of a dream.

The bus turned on to a freeway and flew over a deep crack in the earth. A curved bridge across a bottomless chasm. The glow hit his face as he peered into the District's DownTown.

21

Layers and levels of businesses, housing blocks and rail systems. All hugging the jagged edges of the canyon and criss-crossed by bridges and railings. Hovercrafts zoomed through the air on whirling blue engines powered by magic. The subway system flew by through tunnels and open-air stations. The deeper you plunged, the darker, the more impoverished, the more violent the world became. It was a doorway into hell.

The Underground was the size of Tokyo, New York, London and Shanghai all rolled into one. It was massive, endless and bottomless. The entire ugly monstrosity was built into the hollowed-out stone of the Rocky Mountains and divided into fifty or so Districts.

Millions of individuals all just trying to survive in this dark realm. According to the stats Daniel researched, only about thirty-percent were human.

And Daniel was a new reporter here. He was a reporter in his old life, in the Normal World, the Right Side. Now his boss was a Goblin in a pinstripe suit and pointed blue shoes.

The bus pulled up to a historic site. A courtyard where the Goblin Clans forced out a splinter group of Dwarf nationalists in the 80s. He was staring at the brochure. He didn't notice the girl who walked up beside him.

"Ugly, isn't it?" she said.

Daniel looked up at the bronze statue. The three goblins in trench coats and carrying machine guns stood over a broken Dwarvish anvil. They raised their weapons. He could almost imagine their cackling triumph. It didn't look at all noble or inspiring. *Maybe that's the point?*

He turned to the girl and froze.

Her tiny heart-shaped face was hidden in a huge mess

of thick black hair. She seemed so small, but her big brown eyes seemed to fill up everything.

"Hi," he said, gawking.

She laughed. "Hi!"

♦

Hackers

Three hackers leaned over a single desktop in a dark lab. Sweat dripped down Ben's face and down his back.

"What did you do?!" yelled Jesse.

Ben stuttered. "I... I... I tried to access an aristocrat's account, just a little off the top as usual."

The three made their living off of steal and skimming from the rich's accounts. They could prevent the client notification email. They could break any firewall and cover their tracks.

They were invincible. In the dens of the Underground that meant a lot.

"What happened?!" barked Sam.

The frozen red alert's on Ben's desktop refused and resisted every counter-measure they tried. They were running out of options. They should just wipe the lab's cameras and leave.

"Try this," said Sam, she pressed a few keys in an arrangement that Ben hadn't thought of.

The alert vanished. The desktop returned to normal.

Ben smiled, "Thank you. Close one."

Sam smiled back.

The entire screen flashed red and a high pitched squeal pierced through the speakers.

"Pull it!"

Ben reached under and yanked the power cable.

The screen went black. The only light in the entire lab was the single desk lamp above the computer. Ben and Sam shared a triumphant look and exhaled.

"You saw what it said!?" shrieked Jesse.

"What?"

"… Found you."

A chuckled echoed behind them.

♦

Pathetic

In a dark alley of the Underground a battle raged.

The Dwarf gathered himself from the dirty alley floor. He spat a glob of blood. He grit his teeth and rose proudly to his feet.

Down the alley was his opponent.

Beams of blue light from above illuminated the alley.

The Dwarf, Thryn, stumbled forward teetering on his drunk legs. His addled mind had forgotten what the argument was about.

"Come on," said Thryn. "I can take eight of you!"

The orc crossed his arms. He was a big one. *What was his stupid name?* It didn't matter.

Thryn threw a punch with all his stubborn might.

With a flash of light, he found himself back on the ground. His head rung and his vision swam.

"Fuck you, Greenie," groaned Thryn.

"You're Pathetic, Dwerg."

"Fuck you!" he barked, blood dripping down his nose and into his moustache. "Don't call me that!"

The orc sighed. He had a square head and a squashed nose. The dense green skin across his face twisted into a pitiful frown. He leaned over Thryn.

"You're just another damn dumb Dwerg with something to prove. Go back to the Clan."

The orc left him.

Thryn threw a punch at nothing, screaming and cursing in Dvergr. He collapsed back onto the alley floor and promptly passed out.

♦

Hidden Port

The sea frothed against the cliffs. A churning torrent of ashen grey water, ropes of kelp and slick grey stone.

The ship neared the jagged coast. The water a torrent in the dark grey day. A chugging Peddler galley from the south. It had escaped Cascadian Pirates and a sea dragon off the Mexica coast. A scar across the metal on the ships starboard side remained.

The craggy cliffs were marked with a huge stone plaque. A seaman's marker. It had taken those most of the morning to find it. A hundred feet above the sea, its runic symbols glowed like coals in the wind. A symbol for vessels to approach.

As they neared, Captain Gustav could see how the entrance opened up, almost invisible along the cliffs until in just the right position. His purple coat billowed in the wind, cut in the Franco fashion after his father's ancestry.

The huge opening was like an immense dragon throat.

"Take us in!" called Gustav.

The tunnel swallowed the little chugging galley.

A string of lamps bolted to the tunnel roof was their only guide. The water grew blessedly calm within the tunnel. A canal, stable and unsurprising. After the adventures at sea, the Peddlers were thankful.

Gustav smiled, *finally. The end.*

Eventually, the tunnel opened into an underground port. The cavern walls layered in box-like structures; warehouses, offices and pubs. The old Dwarven architecture with tall pillars and dragon gargoyles. Electric blue lamps blazed.

At the end of the wharf were a trio of goblins. The business. In the gall-ey's hold carried deep treasures of sapphire, rubber and gold. As well as a caged and sedated serpent from the south.

There was a reason dragons had pursued them.

♦

Fire Escape

Claud sat on the fire escape. He swung his furry bare feet. Ma and Pa were arguing inside.

The little boy looked up. Above the alley, way up, was the

ceiling of the Underground. The glowing lights of the city bathed the rocky ceiling flashing multicolored lights. Sometimes the shadows played tricks on Claud.

He kept seeing monsters.

Maybe there really were monsters.

Ma called Pa. "Useless and a liar!"

They lived on the third floor. Claud gripped the bars of the fire escape as he swung his legs. He was seven.

He wished it wasn't so dark here. He didn't like the smell or the food.

He missed the sky.

He got sick a lot more here. He had to stay home last week.

Doctor said he needed vitamins and time under the lamps.

Pa called Ma. "A leech who just watches TV!"

Someone across the alley threw open their window. A big eared goblin with a scrunched face opened his mouth to yell at Claud's parents to be quiet. When the bat-faced goblin saw Claud looking so glum, his lips went tight. He gave Claud a sad smile and closed the window.

Claud sighed. *Everyone is sad here.*

A flying car zoomed overhead on glowing blue wheels. That's when Claud noticed a dark shadowy figure standing on the roof above. A wide-brimmed hat covered her face in shadows but her bright yellow eyes shone through. Black fabric fell from her shoulders to her ankles. She looked like a ghost.

A dark shadowy ghost.

After a moment of listening to Claud's parent's scream, she pulled down her shawl and gave Claud a small encouraging smile. Her long-pointed teeth dug into her bottom lip.

When Claud blinked, she vanished.

Claud just wanted to see the sky again. He sighed.

◆

Swimmers

"Those fucking THOTS!" howled a swimmer.

The den was a jungle of wires and cables. Silver strands and vines going from blocky computer towers. Swimmers made their nests with takeout cartons, drink cans and other un-mentionables.

On each of their heads were butterfly-shaped helmets. Each cyberspaced swimmer was plugged into the internet, drooling and howling with oblivious abandon. They were in the complete freedom of the internet.

Mari glanced around through the forest of cords and reefs of circuit boards to find her partner.

She passed one swimmer tapping invisible keys with nodes implanted in her fingers.

Another swimmer was groping at invisible breasts. His naked body covered in sweat. His underwear wet with god-knows-what.

Mari hurried, trying to find him. She hadn't heard from him in two days. She had tracked his last known location to this den. Mari was dizzy with the noise and anarchic faceless internet addicts. They shrieked, howled, moaned and cried with no conception of their own volume. Their voices and accents slurred by internet slang and energy modifiers.

"Fuck! That's my loot!"

"ROTFLOL! NICE!"

"Come on! Show me!"

"The H33 Hds 144 is so last week."

"Damn gigs make me FUCKING WANT TO SHOOT MYSELF"

"Money transferred. Pleasure doing business with you, dirty girl."

"Post this, cunt!"

"Fuck, WEEB! My Server!"

"OMG! WTF!"

It was like putting your head inside a washing machine filled with bells.

Mari caught a familiar voice through the chaos. A familiar moan.

She circled back to the naked man in soiled underwear and she recognized his moans.

♦

Redecorate

Gunda Brightroar, mercenary, Nidavelliran expat, entered her home. The mansion doors groaned as they opened. The landing was ornate and decorated in the red and marble Gothic aesthetic that drove her crazy. *When will he ever redecorate?* She was strong and wore full body metallic armor.

"The Mistress is back!" buzzed the android climbing down the stairs.

Gunda frowned. Most day's people mistook her for a robot when she was in her armor. Only her ebony face and Afro of black hair showing her humanity. The daughter of a dwarf engineer and an Ethiopian dockworker.

Gunda waved off the android, as its naked female form rushed to attend to her.

Gundra dropped her helmet behind her shoulder. It thunked against the tile floor.

"Simone!" she barked, voice echoing through the mansion.

"The Master is-" chirped the android.

"Shut up!" Gunda marched through the mansion towards the library.

"Simone!"

The android, with her chrome chassis followed behind in quick fidgety steps. "As I said Mistress, the Master is-"

"Simone!" Gunda called through the library. Its high reaching levels dwarfing the half-Dwarf warrior. "Simone!"

"As I was saying, Mistress, the Master is-"

"AHHHOOOOOOO!"

Gunda's eyes went wide. The long wolfish howl echoed through the mansion. Its extended exhale calling on Simone's ancestors; the paintings of 16th century Lycanthrope rebels, 17th century WolfCloaked Colonials and the manuscripts of 12th century Yulfings.

The long history of the Wolf-Vampire conflict was recorded here in these halls.

The howl ended. It always sent a shiver up Gunda's spine.

"Ah, it's his time of the month, isn't it?" said Gunda.

The android nodded.

"I need to pay attention to the moon cycle, in the Underground it's impossible to tell."

"Understood, Mistress, I shall notify you."

"Thank you," said Gunda. "He has three days of this?" Another mechanical nod. "Fine." Gunda began to peel off her armor in pieces, letting it fall hard against the floor until she laid back on an ornate yellow futon in nothing but a tank top and khakis. The android retreated from the library. Gunda sighed, *I love that man, but his monthlies are murder.*

♦

Portraiture

UpTowners always had to show off their wealth. In the higher reaches of the Underground they held lavish parties, galas, public works and partook in the most expensive luxuries. From the lowest CorpLord climbing the economic ladders, to immortal vampiric aristocrats, to Lordling Houses with decades of established rule.

They did anything to show how powerful, charitable and *rich* they were.

Many wanted classical portraiture.

That's where I come in, thought the young artist. Tami Qin dabbed at the shoulder of her subject.

Lady Sireen Clermont sat on a stool with her hands over the book and dagger in her lap.

The lady was stunningly beautiful, soft, curved but powerful, like a ghostly sea goddess. It had been difficult capturing the particular shade of white for her skin, like sea salt; or the exact match of her blue-grey hair which hung around her bare shoulders.

Her black corset and dress were embroidered with silver and sapphire. She already looked like a renaissance painting.

Lady Sireen had sat perfectly still for eighteen hours.

Tami dabbed at the shoulder again, getting the right amount of freckles. Tami's bright yellow eyes danced over the canvas. Her tongue played with her pointed canine.

Neither painter nor subject had any issue of endurance or impatience. The portrait would be finished in one extended sitting. This was a huge client for Tami.

Two month's rent at least.

The room was perfect for this project.

The room was walled with mirrors on all sides. Creating a feeling of eternity going in all directions. It was perfect, neither woman cast so much as a shadow or reflection in the mirror. Just endless repeating images of an empty stool and a brush slowly painting a portrait held by an invisible hand.

A vampire artist painting a vampire duchess in a mirror gallery. Another day in the Underground.

◆

Whole Hog

"Tell me what goes into a meal like this," asked Daniel Chan, reporter for the 10th District's Midtown Tribune, holding up the recorder.

The chef at hand lifted the entire hog by himself. His huge green arms lined with lightning-bolt tattoos. The pale pink carcass crunched against the wire rack. The room was dense with sweet smoke and crackling fires. "It's all in the meat. Can't have some lab grown protein or something half-starved from a cage. I get these from a grower in the Interior."

"Must be expensive."

"Aye, but it's worth it," said Pitmaster Garug. "Business does well enough."

"You're one of the few orc-owned restaurants in the District. Do you feel a level of responsibility?"

"I guess, sometimes, Orcs aren't known for any food culture. But we've always had a wide understanding of what tastes good and what can feed a lot with very little." He scratched his jaw. "My clan, The WildHogs, came from southern Germany originally so you have a lot of basic Euro spices; garlic, bay, marjoram, onions. The crossing over gave us sugar, peppers, and a few other things. From what I was told, we lived south of the Misizipi River until the Thirties. So we learned plenty from the humans there. Then we learned a few things up here."

Garug folded over the wire rack before sliding the beast into the smoker. "Now, it's smoked with Cherrywood coals for about twelve hours. I usually sleep here anyways."

"So would you say this is an amalgamation of orc traditions and southern barbeque?"

"I would. My mentor was human. Good Southron man,

33

skin as black as coal, gave an orc a chance in a kitchen." He moved to the next smoker. Garug opened up the smoker where a golden brown hog split down the middle hissed and crackled.

"Christ that look's good."

"Damn straight it does," said Garug. "So now I take the sauce…" he reached for a mop and a bucket filled with brown-black sludge.

"What's in the sauce?"

"Trade secret."

Daniel raised an eyebrow.

Garug lifted the bucket, offering it to the young reporter. He dipped his pinky and licked off the sauce. Immediately he felt hot burning throughout his mouth. He coughed as the peppery taste went straight up his nose.

The orc laughed, "And?"

"Habanero, Chipotle," Daniel sniffed. "Maple Syrup." he coughed a few more times. "Garlic, onion puree, cumin, paprika, black pepper, clove, maybe a little bit of soy."

"Very good! Now don't you dare tell them the recipe!"

"You get it all fresh?"

"Try to. Garlic and onions are easy, soy too. It's hard to get decent spice down here." He took the bucket and began slathering the inside ribs of the pig. Each dip hissing with flavour and delicious vapour.

"What's your clientele like?"

"Oh, a bit of everyone. Everyone likes good food. I always got young ones with something to prove asking for the Reaper

Chili sauce. Idiots burn themselves a new arsehole." He slapped the sauce over the pig's haunches. Pools of fat and seasoning gathered in the ribs.

"And you just serve the whole hog as is?"

"Yup!" The lid rung when he slammed it shut. He moved to the next smoker. "I'll personally take the beast out for the big table we got on the Patio. Parties only, I ain't wasting this on adventurers. Families, Clans, big parties get this. Otherwise, we just piece it out."

"You do good work here, sir," said Daniel, the deep peppery taste still tingling my tongue. "What keeps you doing this?"

The orc closed the lid. "Oh, it's helluva lot better than mercenary work, which most of my broodbrothers died doing. I'm still here."

"It can't be just safety?"

"It ain't," he opened up a smoker where a huge hog was blackened and crisp. The skin had caramelized like candy from the hourly layers of sauce. He gripped the hog by the haunches and set it on a tray. Droplets of fat fell on the cement floor.

As he backed out of the smokehouse with the hog in hand, he grinned at Daniel, "Orc languages generally don't have a word for hospitality. It's a weird concept to a war society. I love the looks on their faces when they see me with this."

He vanished into the dining room. By the door, a smaller orc flipped ribs, steaks and poultry on a charcoal grill. The smell of the room made my mouth water.

Daniel shut off the recorder. He had all he'd need for this week's piece. "May I have a piece?" The orc grinned and sliced off a chunk.

♦

Party

"The party is wonderful!" shrieked Lady Escal. "Who is your planner!?"

"That's my little secret," responded Baron Careaway, with an especially flirtatious smile.

Lady Escal sipped her chardonnay. "I will find out, my baron, one way or another."

She bolted back into the party. Her gown had made up for that awful laugh. Baron Careaway would have to pursue that avenue for advancement. Escal *did* own a productive auto factory and had ties to the local HighClans. Her court also contained some interesting characters under her patronage.

Careaway looked up, it was a beautiful party and an excellent way to show off his newest addition.

The peak of a mountain had been shorn off and rebuilt with a reinforced dome of glass and steel. Not unlike a golfball, it was built with a repeating geometric pattern for strength and aesthetic beauty. Within was now a sea of gowns and suits. The bourgeoisie of the 17th District. The highest and finest of UpTown.

Beyond the dome was a glorious night sky. The Milky Way high above the Rokki Mountains.

The dome was nearly indestructible, as was Careaway's legacy. As long it endured, so would he. It would survive the worst storms and snow the earth could throw at it. It was a pinnacle of civilized ingenuity. An example of his wealth and power.

He walked through the party like a shark hunting through the shallows.

Nothing can harm me now. Not after his promotion and overthrowing that glutton Romanski.

There was a commotion as he was caught in his thoughts of the permanence of his legacy and power.

Nothing can harm us. He looked up. *Nothing...*

...Is that a dragon?

♦

Outing

Simone took Gunda to a play in the 6th District. A new original play by a mixed Dwarf-Goblin cast. A reconciliation troupe. The politics didn't matter. Gunda was just happy to be out.

Simone was a homebody and an academic. It was a rare treat when he took her somewhere like this.

He wore a red blazer with a black turtle-neck. His line of wolf's teeth around his neck. He made the very notion of a Lycanthrope historian seem respectable. His bristly hair squared off his pale face.

Gunda managed to cram her thick shoulders and even thicker thighs into formal-style bodysuit. She hated dresses. It was hard for her to appreciate formal wear. She felt vulnerable without her armor. A plasma pistol was hidden in her clutch.

She fiddled at the gold necklace around her neck.

Maybe it's too casual? Who wears a bodysuit to a play! I'm a mercenary for the Goblin King. What do I know about-

As if Simone could read her thoughts, he reached over and took her hand. His skin was translucently pale compared to her natural coal-like complexion. He planted a hard kiss on her lips. His bristly lip tickled hers.

"You think too hard," he said. "I can see it all over you."

"Shut up…"

"You look wonderful," he assured her.

"Thanks, babe."

It was hard to find a good guy in the Underground. Gunda was shocked she found hers in a militarized vampire coven. *A half-lycan living amongst vampires.* The Underground was pure madness.

She glanced out the window again, the city past by in a blur of lights.

As arrived at the pillar-shaped playhouse. A crowd of well-dressed folk. One blonde Dwarf with braids waved a protest sign. She was alone and ignored.

Gunda grabbed Simone's hand as they stepped out.

"Thanks."

"For what?"

"For being you."

◆

Purchase

"What… is that?" said Lady Spir, when her husband brought his new purchase into their drawing room. A new toy to show off at the next gala.

"It's quite new, my love!" said Baron Spir with a child-like glee.

The servants had pulled the crate apart, leaning the pile of wood and packing twine in a pile on the black tiled floor.

"That'll show that pompous DownTowner Lupen!" said Baron Spir. "He'll be white with jealousy."

My fool husband things he's a disgrace because he lacks toys… she said to herself. *We are doomed.*

"Its wonderful sweetheart!" she lied. *And a massive waste of funds.* "But what is it?"

She gathered her gown and circled the new toy.

"It's an Automata!" he squealed.

The Technician of the House stepped out of the shadows. He was an Exposed teenager, an impudent child that did not understand courtly manners. Endowed with technical knowledge as a first language by sheer fucking novel luck. *Then he fell into our hands.*

The boy grimaced, terrified of something far beyond his understanding.

Maybe that'll whip him into shape.

A standing suit of bright blue-silver armor, shaped like a beautifully built woman. Between joints were wires and cables. Its chassis of bare metallic breasts, a naval and swooping hips was a homunculi conception of womanhood.

The automata was a serving machine. An ornate rechargeable butler and hostess.

It's face, a polished smiling doll.

Lady Spir grimaced.

◆

Skry Investigations

A knock wrapped against the door.

Karmen had spent almost thirty minutes pacing in front of the door. Its frosted window emblazoned with *Skry Investigations*.

She thought it over and over again in her mind. Standing awkwardly in the train station, in the lobby of the dilapidated apartment block and now in the grimy graffiti covered hallway. Orcs in vests and tank-tops passed by, their arms swirling with red dags.

It had already taken her weeks to decide to make the trip to District 8. It was perfectly safe, just intimidating. A human woman was safer in District 8 than any other District in the Underground.

Huge green brutes and monsters filled every corner. Many fighting, snapping at each other like bored and angry lions. Will this be worth it? Was she sure?

Maybe it was one big mistake.

Could it be true?

Karmen was married to Patrik Rakem. A high ranking CorpLord in District Three. A tyrant of the stock exchanges and UpTown galas.

Karmen hadn't married him for his money and power. He was dashing, romantic and thoughtful. Karmen came with connections, but every sweet nothing, every gesture, every moment of extra consideration didn't seem like a man who could do what she suspected...

She needed to find out.

Had she been so foolish to expect that level of sincerity to be genuine? Had it been real? Could it be true?

The suspected cheating was one thing, but there was something more, something darker, something far viler than she could even imagine. It happened in moments. A glance at his internet history, a peek at his files and phone calls. The odd clients he took on day by day.

Karmen needed help.

She needed someone to investigate her husband.

She stood in front of the door and heard a deep voice growl. "Come in."

Karmen adjusted her clothes. She wore a black dress, cloak and a hat with a veil. It was better to appear innocuous down here. She entered the office.

It was Spartan. Clean, white walls and grey carpet. The back wall was filing cabinets and a colourful bookshelf. A small side table had a coffee maker and a radio that played an old jazz tune. The saxophone wailed.

Behind the desk, the private investigator filled the room with his wide shoulders. A burly brute with the eyes of a hunter. His nose flared as he already gathered her scent. In her nervousness she had worn a heavy layer of perfume.

The orc had scars on his jaw, a stud in one ear and around his collar was a ring of script tattooed to his green skin. His narrow face held in a neutral expression.

Kcaz Skry was, by reputation, a decisive, discreet and effective investigator.

Karmen was as scared of him as she was of the truths he may uncover.

"Please sit down," said the monster, pleasantly. "May I get you some coffee?"

♦

Celebrity

Daniel Chan was always nervous before interviews like this one. It's not the usual 'talk to a popular cook' or 'grab lunch with a playwright or musician' or even 'hang out with an author for an hour.' Even the 'sit awkwardly in a greenroom for an hour' aren't this bad.

This was different.

This was for an artist and activist. Not unusual. Every artist was an activist in some way. Artists had to tune themselves to their own thoughts and feelings as well as the world around them. They can say stupid shit like anyone else, but plenty have more interesting thoughts and opinions than the average reader. *I suppose that just makes them believers, believers in themselves and their feelings rather than actually informed...* He thought back on the horrible interviews with some particularly racist Franco Expats.

He waited in his chair, jacket and tie growing itchy and uncomfortable. He could feel the sweat crawl down his back. He felt like he was wearing sandpaper in a sauna.

The secretary, a nice Black woman with ivory white tattoos across her face, sat Daniel in an office and promptly forgot about him.

The office was simple. Boring grey walls, boring black chairs and a boring grey table. The only dash of colour was a generic flower painting on the wall. Surprising, given the artist's body of work.

Daniel poured himself his third glass of water.

Oh god, what if I need to pee?

He drank the water, more afraid of his voice cracking than the need to run for the restroom.

The thing about artist-activists were that they were common, but when that person is a mega-star-sensation with a P.H.D. and a body of work longer than all of Daniel's articles put together? When that someone is a true auteur? When that person has the ear of District Kings and the vocal critic of the Goblin King.

Someone who had survived threats to her life. A mover and a shaker. A goddam hero with a following with the numbers of a small country.

He was always nervous talking to people like this. *Fuck. I've never talked to anyone like this.*

The door swung open.

He gulped.

A titanic figure stepped in, filling the doorway. An immense green orc squeezed his shoulders through the doorframe. Its huge piggish face looked him up and down. Daniel felt naked and hoped my face didn't hint at his absolute terror.

The beast grunted into the collar of his jacket. "We're clear." The orc vanished and in his place stepped in a woman in a long formless dress and niqab.

She wore sunglasses and had earbuds on. Her dress and veil were black and flowed like shimmering silk. The fabric was lined with two layers of gold. One, a poem embroidered with Persian-style script then bordered with Celtic-Knotwork.

The face of the veil was emblazoned with more Celtic-Knot but spiraled into a Farsi letter.

From between the folds of her niqab sprouted her long pointed ears. They climbed and curled along the side of her head.

She sat down, not looking up from her phone. Her fingers moved in a blur, typing.

Daniel realized he was standing and awkwardly sat back down. He waited for her to acknowledge him, or even meet his eye.

He watched as her fingers typed away for what felt like an eternity. With her veil, sunglasses and earbuds, He felt completely alone.

This is going to be a bad one. He opened my mouth to say something.

"Hold on…" squeaked her voice. She had a deep welsh accent. "And… Just…. About… Okay!"

She cast aside the glasses, phone and earbuds.

The strip of copper-coloured flesh was visible and her deep, inhumanly beautiful, violet eyes seemed to smile at Daniel. Hybrids, he found, as weird a stereotype as it was, always had the most spectacular eyes.

She grabbed his hands from his lap. He realized she was wearing white Victorian-style gloves.

"Thank you for meeting with me!" she giggled. "Thank you so much! It means so much that your paper wanted to do a piece on me. How are you?!"

Daniel was disarmed and managed to smile back. "No! Thank you for taking time out of your day. The privilege is ours."

◆

Slaying

Sergeant Skimore leaned against the wood grain wall flanking the door. Everything reeked of old stain and grease fryers, but now the coppery scent of blood floated in the air. Deep DownTown, they were investigating an apartment block above a strip diner.

Skimore lifted the long silver barrel of his Nailgun. His partner, Gwenlyn, flanked the other side of the door. They could hear giggling inside the apartment.

Gwenlyn was short, stout with braided blonde hair. A proper Dwergi patriot with her Tor Hammer hanging around her neck. She hoisted her own Nailgun and nodded.

Skimore sucked in a breath before kicking open the door. It broke on the lock and swung open.

They rushed into the small, capsule-sized apartment. On the half-kitchen counter sat a girl with her tits out. *If you can call those tits*. Her pale skin and red eyes were usually enough to identify a Vampire.

Her entire mouth was dripping with crimson. A few drops fell to the floor.

A young man, maybe twenty-four, in peak physical condition with dusty blonde hair stood in front of the girl with his hands on her thighs. From a gash on his shoulder a stream of blood leaked down his back.

Gwenlyn grimaced. "Slayers! Hands above your heads."

The girl whimpered, obeying. Holding her arms up while trying to cover her nudity.

The young man, stumbled, holding himself up by gripping the counter. "I let her! It's fine! She didn't do anything wrong!"

"Sir," said Skimore. "We need to ensure you aren't being controlled."

"I'm not!"

Over his shoulder Skimore saw picture on the wall, a piece of street art, both the man and the vampire were drawn and painted in a loving embrace. Skimore begrudgingly lowered his weapon.

Gwenlyn didn't. "There was a murder six blocks from here. A homeless man drained dry of blood. Come with us and we'll hear your piece."

"She's been with me all night!" said the young man.

The girl whimpered. "I'll go. I'll go."

Skimore glanced at Gwenlyn's furious red face.

The girl reached behind her back. Skimore couldn't tell what the girl had. Gwenlyn never waited for a reason… Turns out the girl was just reaching for her shirt…

◆

WitchTrial

"You stand before a court of your peers," said Magus Matthaeus. "A jury of your fellow Magicians, Mages, Wizards and Warlocks. Academics to the Winds of Power."

The accused knelt chained to the hall floor. Arms clasped with silver manacles and circled in a ring of salt. She looked up, her black-blue hair hung stringy around her face, her eyes red and puffy.

Along the walls on benches were hundreds of wizards and other magic users of the 16th District. The center of Institutional Magic practice in the West. In their starry gowns, academy robes, and other splendid uniforms; they looked in horror at the trail of a young and promising magician.

"You stand accused." said the Magus. "Of a most evil murder and the use of black magic."

The accused shrieked. "I'm innocent! I have done nothing!" she looked at her peers. "Those books were for academic purposes!"

"The pentagram? The cyanide?" accused one of the judges. "The blood?!"

Murmurs flooded across the hall.

"An experiment!"

"We have evidence of you infiltrating a 20th District hospital…" said the Magus. "The maternity ward."

The accused hissed. "I haven't left the District in six months!"

The Magus waved his hand. A projector whirled and cast a camera feed on the wall behind the council. A hooded figure with a bundle in her arms ran towards a black Mercedes. The feed froze when her face was revealed under the cowl.

The Magus stood, his voice boomed through the immense chamber. "History is filled with false trials and witch hunts. For too long magic users have been destroyed by the ignorant and superstitious! Only by policing our own can we hope to protect ourselves from the world's flocks and mobs. We alone can protect ourselves!"

Murmurs echoed through the chamber before a single shuttering giggle sent the chamber into terrifying silence.

The accused looked up, laughing, her eyes as black as night as mists of black magic gathered around her.

"I'm never alone…"

◆

Tailors

Daniel Chan was taken into an office overlooking the workshop floor. Dozens of women hunched over sewing machines and tables of leather, fabric and felt.

He sat down with the founder of the workshop, an older white woman with mirror sunglasses, a bowl cut of salt-and-pepper hair and a flamboyant black and gold suit. Laureline Fond had begun her business in 1985. Thirty years prior.

Daniel sat his recorder on the coffee table as the pair both reclined on the couch.

"Ask your questions, sweetie," said Laureline in her sing-song accent.

"Tell me how you began all those years ago?"

"Well…" she whistled. "I was in my twenties when I crossed the Atlantic I was born in a vassalage of AlpenHeim. I had been working here in a laundromat. I lived with four other Saxon girls. One day a couple of clan boys came in to clean their coats of bloodstains. They needed it mended and paid me for the work."

"How did you begin making uniforms?" I asked.

"It just kind of happened. After getting a little extra on the side mending clothes, a clan Boss took me for a drink. Nice goblin, I think he died in ninety-one. He asked what it would take for me to make him a custom coat. I did it on the cheap, but he was so pleased; he gave me a month to outfit his entire Clan. Almost a hundred goblins! All of them wanted something made by me! I was twenty-five and had a huge order."

"And how did you feel at the time?"

"I want to say I was overwhelmed, but I really wasn't. I was thrilled. Focused. I had spent a few years feeling aimless, like an animal trying to survive. I wanted more. They paid half up front and when I realized what I had to do, I quit my job and recruited my roommates. We finished the order with two hours to spare. An entire month staying up late stitching, sewing and cutting, filling already cramped apartment to the breaking point."

"What do you remember about that month?"

"Oh god," she laughed, taking a sip of her glass of golden wine. It was nine in the morning. "It was a blur. I remember being in a routine of sewing and sleeping. I think my roommates kept maki ng this terrible TV-dinner pasta thing just because it was cheap, fast and filling. It tasted like trash."

"Then what happened?" asked Daniel, leaning forward.

"Two other clans almost got into a fight outside my door. They both wanted outfits for their entire clans. At that point me and the girls rented out a small basement and bought a few more machines. Then I made the rules."

"I heard a bit about them," said Daniel, flipping through your notes. "Plenty of clans have rivalries and are willing to go to war for the dumbest of slights. How did you circumvent that?"

"Well, after that first fight, no one died thankfully, I made *the rules*. Duh, duh duhhh," she mimed playing a piano. "My office is neutral ground. No fights. I meet clients here. Business is not to be discussed outside. I will never add body armor or anything extra to the uniforms. They pick what I have in the book. If they want to modify my designs? Fine. I'll cut their ears off if I find out."

"Have you?"

"Maybe," she said playfully.

"How many clans do your provide uniforms for?"

"Oh, about fifty-eight now. I get specialized requests regularly."

"How many Clans still go to war, both sides wearing your work?"

She chuckled, sipping the glass. "Only DownTown Clans really. This isn't the eighties. Streets battles aren't as common as they used to be."

"What happened to your roommates?"

She glanced out the window. "They are running things as we speak. My best friends in the world. To think, I was ready to move out the morning I got that first order. Beatrix was a cocky slut those days and Daniella was a judgmental bitch. Now they are my sisters."

Daniel smiled and allowed the flamboyant seamstress-empress to continue her story.

♦

UpTown Duel

Rapiers whistled through the air. Small side-swords clanged off each other. The Lordlings grunted and swore with each engagement. Their florentine styles proved equally matched.

Their blades locked together. Sweaty faces pressed together.

"You're a fool, Flynn," said Rathbone.

"Yes," said Flynn. "But she's worth it."

"No. She isn't."

They broke apart, catching their breath. The ballroom was

silent. The CorpLords and Ladies, the goblin Bosses, magicians, clerks, adepts, warlords, swimmers and technicians watched with eager anticipation. It was a glorious piece of drama for the 6th District's UpTown bourgeoisie.

All of the regal, wealthy and lecherous eager for blood. Dressed in their suits, frocks and gowns. They were as bloodthirsty as the lowest DownTown fighting den.

The swords clanged as Rathbone and Flynn danced around each other. Back and forth with lightning fast strikes. The only one in the crowd who wasn't enjoying the duel was Madam Rathbone.

"When I kill you," said Flynn. "She'll be mine."

"You really are a fool," said Rathbone. "You think I didn't know? You think you're the only one?"

Flynn dashed back, narrowly avoiding a slash across his throat. His eyes betrayed his confusion.

"I told you," said Rathbone. "She *isn't* worth it. I should know."

Flynn looked towards Madam Rathbone. His beloved, the one he was fighting for. Their hidden love over the past few years had been a light in the darkness of the Underground.

He grit his teeth, his heart wrenching.

All he saw on her beautiful face was embarrassment and disgust. Whatever plans she had for him had evaporated. Everything had been a lie.

Rathbone rushed forward with his rapier.

♦

Chocolate Milk

Daniel Chan got home at about midnight. Not that anyone could tell in the Underground. Alice was usually in bed by now. Tough girl going to med school under patronage had to get her sleep.

Their apartment was in the Southside of the Tenth District. The walls were coppery bricks with dark brown hardwood above and below. It felt like a tomb some days. Daniel went into the kitchen, bathing the sitting area in blue light as he drank half the chocolate milk straight from the carton.

He had considered the whiskey, but the chocolate milk sounded better right now.

It had been *that* kind of day.

Daniel wanted to crawl into bed next to Alice, where he could feel her warmth, her smell, and even those little spasms she had when dreaming. When we first started dating he could barely sleep easy when he felt her body jump mid-dream. He got used to it.

You can get used to stuff like that.

He sat at the cramped kitchen table, sipping the chocolate milk.

The bedroom door creaked open.

Alice came in, rubbing her eyes. "You're home late."

He nodded, not looking up.

"You want to talk about it?"

"You should be in bed."

She sat down. "It's cold."

Daniel managed a half smile. She looked at him from across table. Her hair grew in volume once it passed her shoulders, making her small heart-shaped face vanish deeper into the dense black hair. Her big brown eyes burrowed into his. He knew he wouldn't be able to leave without talking, she had that perfect disarming affect.

"I interviewed a mother who lost her twenty-five year old son," he said before taking another sip of chocolate milk. "He died on a trade mission down south. Supposed to be safe and Clan protected. They forgot pirates don't care about Clan authority."

Alice just let him speak when it got like this. She knew he'd be better getting it out now, than holding it in.

Daniel rubbed his eyes. "So I attended the funeral last week, which was rough. I paid my respects and gave them my card for when they were ready. So the mother poured me a cup of coffee tonight, her voice was still ragged from crying, her face still burned red and her hands still shook.

"She told me about how he was ready to go back to University, how his girlfriend was waiting for him when he came back, how he loved video games and books. He had built his own bookshelf at twelve out of scrap pieces."

He took another sip of chocolate milk. The sweet cool liquid spread through his chest, releasing minimal endorphins to make it all easier. "He is survived by a younger sister and a dog named Rush." My voice cracked. "His mother gave me a few names and associates."

Alice nodded.

"So, my job is easy. I just need to find out why the mission was so important, who died and what it cost a family."

"That's your job, babes," said Alice. "You do it well."

He rubbed his eyes, feeling the ache in my throat. "Doesn't make it any easier."

"No," she stood up and crossed over to me. Her small hand pressed against the back of his neck, her nails digging into his short black hair lovingly. It felt good. "It'll feel easier in the morning."

"Not for the mother."

She leaned down and kissed him hard. Her mouth still tasted of toothpaste. "No, but you know you can't let that stop you."

He exhaled. "No. No, it can't."

"Good," she straightened up. "Come to bed. I'm cold."

He nodded and allowed myself to be led away into the dark bedroom.

◆

The Valkyrie

Explosions boomed on the other side of the doors.

Eardrum-popping thunderclaps interjected by the hard clash of steel and a howling sing-song warcry. A cross between a banshee's shriek and an aria. The screams of Boss Oban's men grew more pathetic with each crash.

The last explosion was followed by a long silence.

Boss Oban leaned forward in his chair. His office was built like a cathedral. A small goblin had to make an impression with a large office. His bejeweled fingers tapped the oaken face of his desk.

Did it really have to come to this? He thought.

He had simply rejected bowing down to a pair of human

upstarts from another district. Now, with insults escalating to violence, they had taken his fortress in a single day. The Valkyrie. The warrior-bard, the half-insane she-wolf that spat lightning and killed warriors by the dozen.

A heavy breath gasped on the other side of the huge double doors at the far end of the gothic-style hall. Narrow pillars and high vaulted buttresses, panes of glass poured artificial sunlight along the chamber.

The goblin Boss waited.

The doors exploded into woodchips and hot metal slag. Oban winced, but kept his composure. Dust hazed the air of the chamber.

In the doorway stood a five-foot-four girl with a mane of raven-black hair. Blue sashes hung off her waist and neck. Her chest heaved and sweat dripped down her mascara stained face.

Her power armor sputtered and hummed. Encased in a Powered Harness, she was a domineering figure of metal and power. Her articulated gauntlets gripped a huge double-bladed axe wreathed in incandescent blue electricity.

Her eyes glowed bright blue.

Despite a bleeding lip, the Valkyrie grinned. "Good Afternoon, Boss Oban. I believe we had an appointment."

◆

Sincerity

The Warlord left a rose on his Valkyrie's pillow.

A simple red rose.

She sat at the edge of her bed after the battle in the 22nd

District. The Warlord was busy ruling his realm. His cavernous holds and tributaries within the Underground. She knew his schedule and responsibilities. He had six meetings today with lobbyists, lunch with a CorpLord from another District and he had to maintain his grip on a rebellious population. *He made the time to leave this for me.*

Her torn jeans and oversized top weren't what a Valkyrie ought to be wearing. She didn't choose the title; it was given to her when she learned how to break kingdoms with an axe. They broke the Yarldoms three years before, now they were breaking the Underground district by district.

She laid back on the bed, holding the rose. Smiling like a teenaged girl and her first sweetheart.

The Warlord, for all his faults, was a sweetheart.

A monstrous, murderous ruler who had to sin to keep the worst of us at bay. In secret moments he could be a sweetheart. It was simple.

She rolled over, staring at the simple memento. Just grinning like the idiot girl she used to be. Before she ruined everything, before she became the Valkyrie.

Maybe it would be okay?

She would be okay.

He was more than the tabloids and newsfeeds called him. He wasn't just a conqueror or a tyrant. He did the best he could with what he had.

And he loved his Valkyrie.

And she would always be his Valkyrie.

♦

PART 3

MUNDUS NOVUS

"The New World"

The Stranger

Her boots crunched against the gravel trail. A black cloak pinned around her neck. A spaulder strapped to one shoulder. Her cowl up, obscuring her face.

The birch and elm trees hung over the trail like the bars of a cage.

It had been ten days since she left the monastery, Chateau de Jean, in south Franco. Her home for five years since her Exposure. Yesterday she passed through Plygate and into the kingdom of NeoAnglia and her journey truly began.

A bird whistled.

The trees rustled. In her peripherals she saw the clumsy shadows of lurking Anglo bandits. Thuggish marauders preying on the forested roads and valleys of the Appalachians.

She was told to begin her journey southwards. She was searching for someone.

The stranger breathed slowly, hardening her heart and relaxing her muscles for the incoming violence.

The bandits stepped out from behind the trees. Wraiths materializing from the shadows of the forest. Calloused hands clutching swords and knives. Ruddy faces with grim expressions and sweat on their brows.

"Hold it," hissed one with a two-handed sword, crouching low like a growling wolf.

The stranger didn't stop.

"Stop!" he snapped. "We saw you in Plygate. Give us your money, your gold, your weapons and we'll think about letting you walk away."

She kept walking, directly towards him as if he wasn't even there.

The man grit his teeth. "Don't make us hurt you."

They surrounded her like wolves around a wounded deer. That was their mistake. She stopped, completely motionless. Her face hidden, only a black braid peeking out from her cowl.

The bandit reached forward for her hood, sword in hand.

The gang moved in.

The instant his fingers touched her hood, metal flashed and his entrails spilled onto the ground. He collapsed in puddle of his own blood, screaming as he died slowly.

In the Stranger's hand, a longsword with a chalky black blade. Completely unreflective in the dim forest light. The crimson dripping from the blade glistened. The silver crossguard emblazoned with the image of wolves leaping from a tear drop.

The rest of the gang charged.

She swung her longsword in a series of brutal arcs, cleaving men left and right. Two charged from behind. She spun on her toes, a bloody arch straight through their necks. Their heads tumbled off into the bushes.

The sword rung between screams. The Stranger swam

through their guards and broke them into pieces. Broken bodies fell in the torrent.

The last man reached for a single-shot pistol. She spun around, snapped up a chrome .45 revolver and fired. The man crumpled to the ground with a smoking hole in his head.

The sword dripped red. She flicked off the blood before sheathing her sword. A trail of blood and bodies amongst the pillars of the forest. The gravel road, a prison for the solitary warrior. Her journey had just begun.

The stranger continued onwards in her search. None would stop her. She had waited too long.

♦

Banjo

The human twanged on his banjo, humming pleasantly to himself.

"… I bless the rains down in… Arizona!"

He giggled, pleased with his tune. He wore nothing but overalls and a straw hat. His feet dangling over the greenish water of the lagoon. Sunburnt skin peeling on his face and shoulders.

The Goblin walked along the creaking boards of the dock. His fingers tapping to the tune, despite himself.

"Good sound you got there, humie," said the Goblin.

"Oh! Well thank ya, Boss. Been playing since I could grip the 'jo only a little after I stopped grabbing at the tit!"

The Goblin nodded. *Grabbing at the tit?* He was always so confused by human biological humor.

"What can I do ya for, Boss?" said the human.

The older human had stringing grey hair poking out beneath his hat. His long arms were thin and his face hawk-like. He was an old man, just enjoying his days fishing and playing his music. Probably going to keep doing that until a neighbour found him dead in his bed.

The Goblin kicked a rock into the lagoon, ripples of water swam across the glassy surface. Dragonflies and crickets buzzed through the air. A falcon cleaned its feathers on a tree above.

"Sorry to say sir," said the Goblin. "Gotta talk about the rent."

"Rent? Squeee... I paid it. All crimped and clean. My Lord does right by me."

The Goblin wore a suit that itched in the southern heat.

He shuffled awkwardly. "Your lord is dead. Dead without issue. The Clans were asked to handle things."

The human cocked his head like a confused dog.

"May I take you for lunch sir?"

"Just tell an old man, Boss."

"The Clans have the Lord's authority and the books don't line up."

The banjo string snapped.

♦

Dunwich

Water sloshed against the great wharfs of Dunwich. The Capital of NeoAngila. The gloomy, mist covered kingdom along the northern Atlantic coast. A land of feuding well-to-do Anglian Houses and isolated Appalachian towns.

The haunting spires and cobblestone streets of the Capital were locked in another long night. Thieves slunk into the wards of the rich, revolutionaries plotted in pubs and the cults of the catacombs prayed for the return of the Old Ones.

From the docks cruised an armored hunting trawler named *The Quincy*. Smoke roared from its smoke stack. Captain Klay, a KrakenHunter, exhaled as he scanned the ocean. *Time for another long night.*

The ocean was as smooth as glass. The moon shined bright in the sky. Beams of white light pierced down into the depths. The perfect night for hunting Krakens.

The Quincy cruised across the glassy plains until the dim lights of the city disappeared.

At the prow of the ship was a rotating harpoon cannon. The sailor gripped the controls with white-knuckled anticipation as he scanned the water.

In the past, Dunwich had been constantly harassed and tormented by Krakens, serpents and other horrors of the deep. Long were the songs of Anglo sailors caught at sea, forced to f ight monsters.

The Quincy headed for deep water. Its spotlight scanned the calm black depths. Without the men and women who patrolled the coast, NeoAnglia would be a landlocked nation. Unable to trade with the riches of West Africa or Europa. They would be locked with only Franco to the north for company.

Klay searched for his prey. The sputter of the engine, the spray of salt, and occasional cry of a gull were the only sounds as the crew waited for fresh terrors. Cutlasses hung on their hips as they went about their duties in silence.

Klay felt his heart pound in his ears. He breathed slowly.

"Sir!" called one sailor.

He saw it immediately. A shadow trailing twenty-foot-long tentacles like a bundle of cables. Just below the surface; a massive Kraken. With golden eyes the size of dinner plates.

Six men set out on a moonlit night. None would return.

♦

HolmGang

Two HallKarls stood at opposite ends of the lonely single street town. The shutters and doors all locked tight against the coming violence. Gusts of dust blew across the gravel road. The wooden faces of the buildings created a tunnel for the HolmGang.

The sun beat down on the tiny Yarldom town.

One HallKarl dropped his gunbelt; drawing his sword as the heavy leather fell to the ground. His sunburnt face was as red as his beard. His sweat drenched brow furrowed. "You're no man."

His opponent, black bearded, drew his own sword and cast aside his revolver. "I'm more man than you'll ever be."

Red-Beard raised his blade, readying himself to charge with gritted teeth.

"Rules?" asked his opponent, who casually leaned on his sword.

"Blades. No guns. No shields. Until death."

Wind blew through the town, slamming one door ajar and tugging at clotheslines. Plumes of dust whistled across the street.

Red-Beard roared, saliva spraying from his teeth. "You did it! I know you did! You killed my sister! You did it!"

His opponent shrugged. "Prove it then."

The Yarl had held s trial and it led to nothing. The Yarl knew what was happening, two of his vassals had set the time and place for the duel. The Gothi has given his blessing. The time for proof and justice was over, now was the time for revenge.

The HallKarls faced each other as equals in the HolmGang. The honour due.

Red-Beard narrowed his blue eyes on his opponent. Sweat dripping off his bright red face.

His opponent grinned through his black beard.

The wind howled. The sun beat down on the small town.

They sprang into action.

♦

Firelight

"What are we going to do?" said one militiaman to the other.

"I... I don't know. The Yarless must have some sort of plan. Her sons will fight with us. There must be something more..."

"You really think so?"

The other militiaman — the older of the two, with silver flecked down his beard and his eyes full of fear — considered the question. He said, "No. I don't."

They both looked out from the town walls.

Across the dozen miles of farm plots and pastures at the edge of the forests to the north, hung dozens, maybe hundreds of firelights. Each glowing with warm threatening light.

The message was simple.

New Rekvik was completely outnumbered and reinforcements were unlikely.

"What can we even do against Whistling Jack?" said the younger man.

The older man shrugged. "Not much. The Skraelings are many and they have good reason to fight."

The younger man scoffed. "They need to get over it."

"Oh, should they? The lands of their forefathers were taken from them. They have good reason to want it back."

"Our forbearers lost their homeland!"

"We lost our homeland by the grace of the gods. You want to fight Tor himself for Eastland? You want to return to an island of volcanos and rocks that you've never even seen before?" The young man didn't say anything. "They know who took their land. They can look at each town and count. They can look us in the eyes or down a rifle's sight to see who took their land."

The wind howled over the wood and steel battlements.

The older man exhaled. "We did."

◆

Peddler

We are an essential part of this world, thought Soef Fettirsson, as he cracked the reins. The pair of heavy draft horses lumbered on. They were more reliable than a vehicle in this world. Gas was for the rich. A horse was a man's friend.

It could get sick, was less powerful and could be injured, but the companionship and versatility made the difference.

Fuel was too expensive anyways.

Soef's purple coat held back against the wind. The wagon crawled around the mountain trail. Dense sloped forests flanked the road.

Next to Soef sat a young Skraeling man. Nice boy. *For a Skraeling.*

His light brown face was covered in stubble. A heavier lad, but his brown eyes were as quick and perceptive as a goblin. He wore coat and trousers of denim.

His bag and case carried electronics, a computer and a hundred odd devices and components.

One of those technicians. Probably Exposed in the last few years.

Maybe Soef's bias was against the boy's profession. He was the competition. With the NewTech, peddlers had to struggle to learn things they could never understand. The internet, phones, cellular, bandwidth… Soef shuddered. He was old and hunched at this point, with wisps of hair around his ears. A black cap on his bald head.

Or was he?

Soef traded in goods, luxuries and the world's tangible pleasures. He never touched modern tools and electronics. The world would always need hardware, salt, sugar, tobacco and handmade toys.

The wagon rumbled around the curved trail.

In the distance, there was a river valley. A small village in its depths with a mill and tendrils of fireplace smoke. Above the village, overlooking like an ugly monster was the local's Yarl's keep. The tower of a forgotten Dwarf outpost with newer Eastlander's expansions of stone and wood.

The peddler in his purple coat would sell is wares to the people while the technician set up a phone line and computer for the Yarl and his sons.

♦

The Shade

The sun bled through the canopy of flowering crab-apple trees. The low-branches gave the glade an enchanted feeling. On a bench sat a girl. A proper southern aristocrat's daughter. Around her feet piled pedals from the trees. The cicadas rustled around the orchard.

She wore a flowing white dress. The sun bit into her already sunburnt skin. Her chestnut hair fluttered in the wind.

She sat adjusting the lenses of her camera. The strap dug into the back of her burnt neck.

She crouched onto the grass, feeling the prickle of the grass on her front. Using her antique Polaroid camera she was making art. Her mother disapproved. A good girl doesn't have frivolous hobbies.

Become the daughter we need you to be, chirped her mother's voice.

"Get married," she grumbled as the shutters clapped. "Run the family estate."

She stood up. *Never.*

There was a rustling in the glade. Her hand dropped to the small knife she had hidden within the folds of her dress.

From between the low trees stood a man. She recognized him. One of the workers. One of the union leaders, one of the radical ones.

He was naked, except for a thin shift around his waist. His broad chest covered in bloodstains and cuts. His deep dark brown skin shone with sweat. Powerfully muscled from work on her family's estate.

He looked exhausted, hurt and in pain. His hansom face covered in a look of both shame and terror. A huge claw mark scar across his right bicep.

The girl caught her breath.

I have to get him out of here. If the guards see him...

If her mother found out...

♦

Gardens

Duc Rubais sat on a stone bench along the quiet green pond. The gardens always helped him think. Fronds, reeds and blossoming trees surrounded him. It was a grey day; a diplomatic guest had come to the capital. The Goblin Clans to the west had sent a young woman as a representative, small and mouse-like, but far from meek.

The Royal Court was both terrified and shuttering with fascination. A vampire had been sent into their midst. *A tamed one supposedly.*

The Duc tapped his foot. The breeze shimmered the green pool, the crisp air bit through his regal uniform.

Rubais watched a turtle laze about on its rock. A clutch of geese had flown into the gardens and glided across the water.

On the glassy field of lily pads sat two small Fae. The creatures were always welcomed. Small, intelligent, tricksters with power beyond mortal comprehension.

Once, Franco Christians had hunted Faefolk like vermin.

Fanatical fools.

Now they were to be respected, cherished and given offerings. *Horribly pagan*, thought Rubais, *but a blessing.* Woe the Franco or any mortal who disrespects the Faefolk.

The two sat conversing, little more than whispers like wind chimes.

One was pale, winged like a butterfly and female. A tiny colouration in the line of a dress. A fuzz along its face and two big diamond eyes.

The other was a dark brown colour, like red clay, with black tendril hair down its back. No wings, only a tunic of interlaced grasses. Its big black eyes full of light.

They talked in two different patterns, then after a moment, they switch into the other's pattern.

The Duc leaned back, realizing that they were teaching each other their language. *Brilliant.* He got up, an idea arose in his brain on how to move forward with this guest.

♦

Dumplings

There were nine temples in Fjordheim. A riverside town filled with sacred places, cults and small shrines. Pilgrims of dozens of denominations traveled to this place. That also attracted all manner of peddlers, hustlers, travelers and mercenaries. *Godly trails rarely brought godly men.*

And they all needed to eat.

The Bacchian Temple provided the best food and in the most quantities to any who asked.

The Apollonian temple healed, the Temple of the Goddess loved, the Rage Temple battled. All paled in comparison to the Cult of Gluttons in sheer popularity.

Brother Bao had come to the cult from the East. Not the Far East. *That was even more west from here.* Just eastwards from the Yarldoms. He had traded a comfortable monastery for a land filled with monsters and barbarians. His old temple was too strict and forgot the greatest joy a person can give.

A decent meal.

I just need to feed people, he thought, his wide jolly face always rested with a smile. He stood apart from the Greco and Latin monks. He was still a Buddhist monk. They enjoyed him. *Probably because my cooking is better.*

He sat at a table beneath the temple. The air warm with the sweet smells of stored food. On the table sat two bowls. In one bowl, a pink mush of pork, chicken, onions, cabbage and corn. Seasoned with salt, pepper, garlic, homebrewed soy and what little sesame and ginger he could grow himself. Or buy from the Peddlers at extortionate rates.

The other bowl had a rich paste of gelatinized chicken and pork broth.

Across the table was a junior monk, Nikan, rolled out small disks of dough. A young Greco boy with curly brown hair and a natural tan. *The local girls must love him.* Good thing the Bacchian cult celebrated indulgences in all their forms.

Brother Bao filled each dumpling and pulled it into a perfect roll with an exact number of pleats. He placed it in a birch bark basket for later steaming.

It was a quiet, calming and methodical task.

The Brothers of Bacchus enjoyed it. *Make due with what you have, feed the hungry.* That was the only divine tenet Brother Bao accepted.

◆

Orchard

Chieftain Usueg's gardens were indeed beautiful. Spiralling rows and trails of titanic spruce, pines, oaks and hardy sequoias. It wasn't the delicate gardens of the Franco nobility or the opulence of the UpTowns of the Underground. NeoAnglia could not afford such luxury.

It was a place of worship, ancient tribal royalty and rugged beauty. As close an imitation of the Chieftain's homeland as could be managed.

The Chieftain sat on a stone block and bid Lord Janis to sit.

Lord Janis and Chieftain Usueg, men of power, decisions, regality and the Sword of Damocles.

They sat along a perfectly round pool. The water like black glass at the base of an especially huge sequoia.

"Beautiful, isn't it?" said the Chieftain, his voice as harsh as storm winds.

He was eight-feet tall. A Jotunn from beyond the seas and snow. A long way from Jotunheim, but assuredly as powerful and respected as any lord of this continent.

"Aye, it is," said Lord Janis.

"My clan came to this land as traders on a single longship. I grew up on this continent, but I always felt trapped. Caged in the land of smallfolk," he exhaled. "This place helps."

His boulder-like fist rested on his knee.

"You are your family are assuredly mighty and wise," said Janis. "I am honoured to share in your company."

The Chieftain shifted on the boulder. He wore a wrapped tunic of fine cotton and furs, pinned with a sabre-tooth broach. His face was as heavy and worn as the sequoia bark.

"I know the Undergound is a realm of colourful cloth and wagging tongues. I imagine it helps in the dark, but this is not some tunnel." His black shark-like eyes narrowed. "Cut the crap. What business would you like to discuss with a Jotunn Chief."

◆

Poet

They don't know how it approached the city without being detected. It avoided being seen from the coast all the way inland. Through rivers and tributaries and across Ducies and Baronies. It was already on the walls, and out of the reach of cannons, before the garrison realized what was happening.

The creature was unknown to the scholars and scientists of the city Soeur Perdue, The Lost Sister, Capital of Franco. Neither crocodilian, serpentine or dragonoid. Eight squat legs on a long-scaled body, a long snapping head with fibrous crests and fangs dripping in hissing venom.

The Franco poet, Leyel Leclerc, leaned back. He sat in a small off-street diner. The mahogany walls dressed in antique paintings. Leyel was no reporter, the facts he had were second-hand and likely to be inaccurate.

He was a poet. Everything he touched had an air of theatrics and pretension. It didn't matter. He would say what he had to.

A beast from the south pushed far off course for some unknown reason. Some say the warming of the climate, others say a curse, others say it was called by the catacomb cults. In any case, Franco couldn't even pronounce its traditional Maya name.

A truck bustled by on the cobblestone street. The tall waitress placed a cup of tea for the poet. She had big blue eyes and a white frilled blouse.

The beast slunk over the walls, just as the garrison sounded the alarm, and dove into the Studio District. The beast tore through a theater, a gallery, three stores and a housing block before it was slain by the authorities.

The Knights and Slayers drank themselves into a victorious hangover.

It had been too late for the District. It had been too late for the apartment block. It had been too late for Leyel's wife, Catrin.

He slammed his pen deep into the paper, ink bleeding into the page.

◆

Ranchers

The Hadrosaur herd splashed through the river. Each scaly beast almost eight meters long with heavy hoof-like feet digging into the muddy riverbed. Their crests and horns flushed a low orange, showing a calm and focused herd. Their trumpeting calls echoed for miles across the badlands.

Harrington watched the crossing from atop her horse. Her ruddy face shaded by the brim of her hat. She cracked her bullwhip, urging the beasts forward. They needed to hurry. The next leg of the journey was always the dangerous one.

"Harrington! Harrington!" called another cowboy, Barry McDougal. He rode up fast, clutching his hat.

"What is it...?" *This ought to be good.*

"We got trouble sir!"

Oh god, now what?

The pair rode away from the herd. Harrington saw Barry draw and begin loading his repeater. She took the clue and began doing the same.

On the crest of a nearby hill stood Rex Walsh atop his mount. The horned theropod stood a meter over the heads of the horses. The giant predator panted, its serrated jaws dripping saliva. The horses shied away from the monster.

"We got trouble," said Rex, from the saddle on the theropod's shoulders. He pointed with the barrel of his AK-47.

Over the next rise, across the patchy grasslands, was a collection of dark figures. Huge black scaled Theropods. A pack of almost a dozen apex predators. Each as big as Rex's own monster.

Harrington grit her teeth. "They're after the herd." She kicked her horse into a gallop. "Come on!"

They signaled to the rest of the ranchers the danger.

The pack of monsters split and charged towards the herd.

◆

Kraken vs Titan

Along the Carolinian coast, a battle raged beneath the

black waters of the Atlantic. Night had turned the ocean into a plain of perpetual darkness. A war between ancient oceanic demons silent to the world.

A beast from the southern seas had found itself pushed northwards more and more each season. Forced out by stronger rivals, human pollution and deeper evils of the Atlantean trenches.

The titan drifted along the Florida mangroves feeding on the few dolphins, sharks and sea cows it could find. Only once did it risk foraging on the shore, slacking its immense hunger on a cattle ranch.

A Kronotitanus. A warm-bloodied reptilian titan of primordial heritage, with webbed claws for hunting on land as well as the coastal seas. As vicious a monster on land as it was at sea.

It followed the coastal currents, letting its mind rest. Floating half-unconscious by adjusting its hydrogen glands. An organic buoyancy tank, similar to that of Dragons for flight and fire. It breeched with a jet of water from its nose as it caught a fresh lung of air before cruising back into the depths.

Its bulk blocked out the beams of starlight from above. Its tail swaying slowly.

It didn't notice the ribbon-like tentacles reaching from below. The long sucker-lined limbs of a truly enormous kraken.

The cephalopod monster mistook the titan for a whale or a ship. What delights it could find within an oaken hull?

Its arms surrounded the sleepy monster. Each sucker lined with toothy barbs.

Its many arms snapped tight around its prey.

The titan's red eyes burst open. It roared as tentacles wrapped around his body, pinning its limbs. A jet of superheated water escaped from its mouth. A tentacle wrapped around its jaws, clamping its long snout shut.

The tentacles dug into the titan's fleshy underside, creating ribbons of black blood. The barbs scraped against the volcanic scales of its back.

The kraken had realized its mistake. This was no defenceless whale. This was no sweet treat of sailors. It knew it had to drag down the creature and drown it. The jets along its mantle fired water, jerking the deadly embrace further into the black darkness.

The titan wrestled in the abyss, trying to free itself, thrashing its tail. The kraken continued to pull it further down. Pressure began to hammer the coastal predator. Its oxygen reserves depleting faster with each meter descended.

It flexed its diaphragm as decades of hunting experience had taught it. Its hydrogen glands expanded on what little remained in its stomach. The pair began to rise, helped by its thrashing tail.

The kraken began to constrict, chocking the rival monster.

The titan's arm slipped from the tightening embrace. A webbed claw cut through the water. Slashes appeared on the kraken's fibrous black mantle. A plum of ichor filled the water. Its eyes, the biggest in the world, flashed with fear. It struggled to chock the life from its rival.

With its freed limb, the titan pawed at its snout, slashing through the tentacle. The kraken's eyes snapped wide.

The kraken drove its razor-sharp beak into the titan's side. A cloud of blood swirled around them. Jaws free, the titan let out a silent roar. Water began to fill its lungs. It would drown and fall into the unending abyss of the Atlantic

It dug its claws into the fleshy mantle of the kraken and bent it towards its jaws. Superheated water fired from its mouth. Its hydrogen glands deflated, a magical-alchemical reaction exploded within the titan. The water bubbled and the skin of the kraken peeled back. Layer by layer burned away like acid eating at its flesh.

In their twirling embrace, the monsters vanished cloud of blood, ichor and ink.

When the chaos cleared, the titan burst upwards, desperate for air.

A chunk of the kraken's mantle in its claws.

It would eat well tonight.

The titan burst from surface. A black-blue and white rocket and arrow-shaped snout. It let out a wailing roar before crashing back into the water.

♦

Mudstained

The storm raged overhead. Flashes of light in the carpet of dark grey clouds. The western badlands stretched in all directions. A wasteland of sparse prairies, desolate deserts, wanderlust skies and craterous canyons. The mesas like guards standing resolute in the open plains.

The great mountains always visible in the distance like a blue serrated saw blade.

Rain began to patter the cracked soil.

Storms in the badlands were few and far between.

Settlements became ghost towns as people fled for shelter. Ranch camps staked down their tents or moved to high ground. The great wandering herds of antelope, bison and hadrosaurs huddled for warmth. Their breath coming in jets of steam.

In the depths of a forgotten canyon, the waters began to rise. At just the right time and level for an awakening. A birth. The rise of a brutish lineage. Lightning flash, revealing that the stone walls were emblazoned in the images of beasts and prehistoric monsters.

An unholy birth began.

The mud began to bubble and churn. The newborns writhing in their fungal wombs, locked in hibernation until the right conditions were met.

At the entrance of the defile, a great tribe gathered. Broad grey-green shoulders pattered with rain, water sliding off their heavily muscled backs. Their steaming breathes created a mist in the air. There were hundreds of them.

Lightning flashed.

The mud continued to churn until limbs became visible. Mudcaked arms broke from the earth's embrace. A single clawed hand reached upwards as pre-programed instincts drove the newborn upwards. Climb up. Up. Up. Up. Find air. Breathe.

More arms broke the surface. A horrifying garden of writhing limbs in the water and mud.

Finally a head broke free. Pointed ears, a squashed nose and square jaw. A fanged maw let out a roar with a gust of steam, clearing its throat of mud, like a crying baby clearing it lungs.

Soon a new generation of Mudstained rose out of the soil of the badlands. Dozens of brutish orcs, sniveling goblins and bent-back gremlins. They howled and thrashed, clumsy as newborn foals.

They will learn, thought the Lord of the Mudstained.

Their tribe, their clan, watched from above. Drumming

grew as the newborns struggled to life. If one was trampled or drowned in the mud, they did not deserve to live. They lived by the law of nature. Survival of the fittest.

As the newborns stumbled by pure instinct to the familiar scent of their clan, the Mudstained let out a roar of triumph. A chorus of cries and songs. Greetings for their brethren.

At rear of the clan, watching the process, was the Lord of the Mudstained. *They would do.*

At her side, a huge horned-theropod. Its back and tail as rocky as the badlands. The reptilian creature reared its devilish head and roared. Its serrated jaws split as if to swallow the flashes of lightning.

♦

Angelics

The species is a mystery. Homo Sapiens Angelus, wrote Leyel, his third pen bled dry and his fifth cup of tea drained.

Known across the world under as many different names as there are languages and in as many forms. They continue to baffle and astound scholars and mystics of the highest orders. Government reaches into their communities have always been met with a respectful expulsion followed by the group vanishing.

Leyel sipped his lemon-ginger tea.

Winged humans.

Immortal? Unknown

Powerful? Likely

Dangerous? Unknown

They possess magics and knowledge unknown to men and dwarves.

As with all the major sentient races; humans, orcs, goblins, dwarves, giants and all forms of beastfolk, Angelics are twisted into the myths and legends of the Right Side.

Angelics share a remarkable solidarity across world cultures in keeping their secrets.

Leyel tapped his pen. He had spent much of the day and evening at the table in the off-street bar. He was lost in writing. Was it poetry? History? Science? He didn't know. He just wrote what he knew to be true and acknowledged the limits of his academic knowledge.

Rumors linger of their immortal divinity, similar to the aelfen of North Europa and other mystic beings. Tied deep into magic. As the modern scientists call it; Veiled Radiation.

Those are the concerns of the Franco Academy of Magics and other sorcerer institutions.

Further tales the existence of places of legend as real, civilizations and cultures unbound by the earth. Knowledge beyond us groundlings.

Asgard? Heaven? Shamballa? Olympus? Leyel smiled, exhausted. *Laputa?*

Rainbow bridges and forgotten magic!

He set down his pen.

What was he to this? He was a poet... or maybe now a chronicler of sorts. What did it matter? These mystic beings.

♦

Overlook

The stairway clutched the cliffs rising out of the dense forest canopy. The ancient steps led to a series of switchbacks, then higher into the gapping mouth of a cave. The floor smooth and polished, overlooking the seemingly endless valley of autumn colours.

Matis threw off his hood. A single figure in a brown cloak. He was greeted by four others in brown cloaks. They surrounded a fifth crooked figure in a blue cloak. An exceptionally tall and stubbornly old man threw back his own hood. His stringy white beard reached past his naval.

Matis kneeled. "They are coming, my Master. They have new allies."

The Master sighed. "Our time is up. We must prepare." He cast a leering yellowed eye at Matis. "Thank you, brother."

Thank me later, you piece-of-shit. The hooded figures fled into the cave. Their hideout for many years.

An arm reached out and grabbed Matis from the shadows. He was pulled by the collar into the shadows. Lips slammed into his.

He knew who it was and leaned into it.

He could smell pine on Cesare's clothes.

They broke their embrace.

Cesare smiled up at Matis. His brown hair in a mess. His face seemed to say. *I missed you.*

Matis *did* miss him. He really did. His chest jumped into his throat. Matis swallowed and wished the fates had been kinder to them.

Soon I'll betray the cult to the authorities... And Cesare with them...

♦

Lookout

The pair of militiamen lay in a hidden sniper den. The land was perfectly flat. A horizon of white snow and black spike pines. They had a good view of the road along the small stream. It wasn't a commonly taken route.

"Why are we even here?" groaned Sean, wrapping his wool blanket tighter. His red beard sprinkled with frost.

Murphy ignored his compatriot.

"Can't believe we have to stay out here until Monday…"

Murphy was getting annoyed with the belly-aching.

"We could be-"

"You want our Yarl flanked? You want raiders on our asses?!"

"No one comes here!"

"They might. One day when they do, the Yarl will be thankful he had two warriors watching his back. So just shut up."

Sean did, he chewed his lip as cigarettes were not allowed.

Murphy returned to viewing through his scope. Careful not to touch his eye to frosted metal.

Beyond the lookout position was the frosted stream. Cold water still rushed over polished stones. A few naked trees grew sparsely in the field before the dense forest in the distance. Tuffs of frost bitten foliage and grass shuttered in the wind. The white, blue and pale green terrain was picturesque in its simple beauty.

Murphy gasped. "Oh no."

Shadows moved in the forest. They just appeared from between the trees. They were moving fast towards the lookout.

He cocked the rifle.

"Get the radio!" he screamed.

There was a thud atop the den.

♦

A Tower

Margaret had been exiled from the Franco Colleges of Magic a long time ago. Her hair had gone silver in that time.

Ever since she had lived in a lonely tower in the mountains. Technically she was a vassal of Duc Levis. She owed him tax and tribute. She offered him illegal use of magic and healing. That gave her the isolation she desired until her overlord required her services.

She sat in her tower thumbing through a tome when her console beeped. She may be isolated, but she kept up to date. Internet and a computer had been a gift from the Duc after a particularly embarrassing scandal.

Margaret slid over. Outside the tower, thunder crashed. The forecasted storm had arrived. The tower apartment was warm and homey. Decades here had turned an exile's dungeon into a home.

She answered the video call.

Her acquaintance, Zelda, appeared. A blonde-haired girl calling from all the way across the continent in the Rokki Mountains. The realm of the Goblin King. A young apprentice in the magic college there. *An entire District dedicated to magic. An entire underground city…* that was a thought.

More thunder rumbled.

"Marg! I found it!"

"Found what?"

"I found what the Magus has been hiding. What all of them have been hiding! What they all refuse to show us!"

"Breathe girl!" chuckled Margaret. Zelda was thirty years her junior, but the young mage was a dear friend and a useful contact. "Tell Mama Marg what's got you in a fix?"

The girl breathed. "I talked to a few other known radicals and a few other…" the girl caught herself and blushed.

"Exiles," said Margaret. *There's no denying what I am.*

"Yeah," she squeaked. "And I found it!"

"What?"

"Information on Demonology! I knew they were hiding it!"

Lightning flashed through the window.

♦

Monstrosity

Heller ran through the dark city street, feet splashing in puddles. His heart pounded as he desperately tried to escape. He yanked on every door handle, but nothing gave and no one came to help him.

The shudder of groaning metal echoed overhead.

He whispered a prayer to the Christ God. He hadn't prayed since he was a child. Funny how desperation and terror bring the godless to the chapel. It was pointless.

If there was a God, it wouldn't have created *that*.

That horrible monstrosity.

He had seen something he wasn't supposed to in the catacombs. He had run. He had seen the collection of robed men. Their shadowed faces lost in blasphemous tribute.

He ran harder. The night sky flashed with lightning. A shadow dashed over the alley.

The rain hit hard.

Water pattered against Heller's face. The cobblestone alley grew slick.

He slipped.

Of course, he had.

The rain slicked alleyway was frightfully dangerous.

He hit the cobblestone hard, sliding on its wet surface. He groaned, feeling pain web across his body. He clutched his bruised elbow, feeling numbness climb up his arm.

In the catacombs, we saw the men in robes, illuminated by only candle light. Similar to the city's cathedrals, but gave none of the warmth or mercy. This was the opposite. This was wrong.

Between the robed figures was a dead girl. Her face covered in bruises and scars. Her shabby clothes and scabs told Heller she had been a street addict. Someone easily lost and forgotten, easily taken for nefarious purposes.

Heller clambered to his feet, but it was too late. A flurry of groaning metal echoed behind him, like the creak of an old door.

He looked back, but was struck in the head. In his lingering consciousness, he felt himself picked up by the throat. He could smell harsh metal and sour rotten flesh. He gasped, the putrid smell flooding his mouth.

He felt the hand, hard and skeletal, like mechanical brass fingers, but covered in something cold and fleshy. He opened his eyes and screamed in horror to see a face of writhing interlaced hands before it swallowed his whole world.

♦

Quiet

The waters of Peg, so still, the blue horizon disappeared into the sky. The gentle chirp of birds and coo of a loon echoed.

The shieldmaiden kneeled on the rocky short. Pebbles and shells crunched under the weight.

"It's so quiet," said her companion.

"Yes," said the shieldmaiden. "It makes me uncomfortable."

"Why?"

"Stillness bothers me. The quiet before a raid, the silence of the forest before a great bear attack." She rose.

"You're being dramatic, besides," said the companion. "*We* are the ones attacking."

The shieldmaiden stood in silence.

Along the curve of the shore were seven motorized raiding vessels. The metal and plastic of their hulls painted black. Along the railings were slabs of steel. The prows painted with dragon eyes. The descendants of the longships of yore.

The shieldmaiden sighed. "Let us begin."

She turned to her band of forty warriors. Her chest armored in Kevlar and scraps of metal. She raised a sword.

"Onward Eastlanders! Let's show the swine who's in charge!"

♦

PART 4
DISTANT REALMS

*"Endless as the sky, Jotunheim, Nidavellir, Hellas, Mali, Mexica
and beyond. From the peaks of mountains to the depths of the
blackest abyss."*

Unicorn

Wind whistled across the frozen steppe. Wisps of grass flickering across the rolling landscape. The endless blue sky stretched unblemished from horizon to horizon.

Jhonas wiped the back of his hand across his boulder-like face. His thick eyelashes blinked away any dirt that blew into his face.

He zeroed in on his prey. It had been a long week of tracking. Now he saw the lumbering target in the distance.

Jhonas moved quickly to cover the distance. His tree trunk-sized legs carried the young Jotunn across the landscape.

His long-barreled cannon in his hand. The firearm tipped with a shining steel spike.

His breath streamed across his face. His black hair flying in the wind.

Downwind. Perfect.

He moved fast. By the time the fat unicorn turned its shaggy brown head, he was already in position. The beast's great blubbery shoulders dripped with condensation. It's immense ridged horn sprouting high from its low hanging head. Its coal-coloured face housed its dumb little eyes. The unicorn snorted.

The cannon aimed from a crouch; Jhonas fired.

The blast rumbled across the steppe.

The unicorn fell sideways. Its spine severed behind the head. Blown out by the shot.

Jhonas smiled at the clean kill. Food, fur and ivory. A good kill. He pulled back the bolt, releasing the shell and catching it. The brass was hot in his calloused hand. He glanced at the sky. *Gods bless the gift.*

He rose from his position.

His nose flared and he realized he wasn't alone. He could hear the muffled paw steps closing in around him. He turned. A pack of six spotted Steppe Lions surrounded the young Jotunn. Their sabre-like fangs bared and dripping.

They hid downwind and hunter had become prey.

He was not some helpless dumb animal. He growled, raising his bayonet for the incoming attack.

♦

Griffon

Aqi sat by a pool. Her porcelain white legs swaying over the blue-green water. The gurgling of the spring and the rustle of the forest gave the immortal all the solace she required. Eternity was her only true companion.

Her naked form equal to any goddess.

A nymph, a creature of the forests and pools. She stroked her long green-chestnut hair hoping to attract her prey. Her long hair fell down her back and over her breasts. Her warm oval face and intense blue eyes glanced around the glade.

Her naked form had brought a many mortal into her grips.

They had always been quite delicious.

A rustling behind her told her she would eat well tonight. She turned but her face fell from seduction into complete horror. It was no wandering shepherd or willing adventurer. A great lion had managed to sneak up on her.

The golden beast's mane was like brass and its eyes like polished amber. A black clawed paw took a step forward. It sprung off its powerful legs, white sabre-teeth and claws drawn.

Aqi had no time to flee, no chance to dive into the pool. Only a whimper at her eternity's end.

A shadow crashed through the canopy.

A great eagle slammed into the lion. A maelstrom of fur and feathers, brown and gold, claws and talons. A deafening roar and howling screech as they tore into each other, blood splattering the forest floor, defiling the enchanted glade.

Aqi dove into the pool, away from the battle.

When she rose out of the pool at the end of her breath, it was quiet. Clear water ran down her shoulders and white skin. The lion was dead. It's golden fur criss-crossed with crimson. It's throat a mess of red.

The eagle, sat equally bloodied, but alive and very hurt.

Aqi rushed to its side. With all her strength she helped it crawl to the water's edge. She then began spooning the water into its bronze-coloured beak.

◆

They're Coming

…It wasn't dread or fear. Just quiet resignation.

The scout stood in the space between two huge oak trees. His bow strung over his shoulder and elfin face held neutral.

"Thank you," said Stalwart. "Report to your captain."

The scout nodded and vanished. As if he evaporated in the wind.

Stalwart looked up to his sister. Leaves and pedals danced through the glad in the spiralling breeze. She floated fifteen feet in the air, meditating. The smell of pure simple magic hung in the air. The confetti of foliage twirled around her as she descended.

She stepped back to the ground as easily as stepping off a chair. She blinked, "You know we can't possibly win."

"I know."

"And if we lose, they will cannibalize this world and leave it a hellscape. A husk where life will *never* grow back."

"I know, Elas. I know."

"You are our king. What can we do?"

Stalward rubbed his jaw. "What can we do?"

"We can't bleed them, a thousand more rise each moment. We can't stop them, they are beyond mortality."

"So are we."

"It doesn't matter! We are going to die!" Pain layered her voice.

Was it hopeless?

"I won't give up. We can't. There's just too much to lose."

"Then what is your plan?"

"It has acted with purpose. Its landfall shows higher planning. It has a mind and intelligence. An intelligence can be communicated with."

"You want to talk to it?"

Stalwart shrugged. "What else do we have to lose?"

♦

Merchants

On the horizon, the crew glimpsed three black specks, tiny black flies on an emerald blue canvas.

Officer Tek looked to his Captain. "Sir? What are they?"

"I don't know."

They adjusted their heading fifteen degrees to the west. The next morning, the three specks still appeared on the horizon. They had been seen.

"What are they, Sir?"

"I don't know," said the Captain. "But they've seen us."

They were a merchant ship, *Dragoon*, coming from the Carib-Republic of Saint Baptiste. The hull packed with frozen fruit, spices, rum and sugar. High priced goods for Vinland and NeoAnglia. The risk of such an extended journey was more than worth it given the prices.

By the next morning, cold winds blew hard from the east and the black ships were still on their trail. There could be no doubt they were pursuing us.

"Shit…" whispered the Captain.

"Sir?" asked Tek.

"How far are we from the closest port?"

I checked our heading with the Carib Helmsmen, he shook his head. Sweat beading across his brow.

"Two days, sir."

"Can we make it?"

Another calculation followed. All crew members in the cabin watched with silent worry. "Maybe. I don't know sir."

The Captain wiped his face with the back of his hand. He was trembling.

"Orcs…"

"Are you sure?"

He nodded. The helm was as silent as a crypt.

Orc Pirates didn't just search for prey to loot, they wanted people to fight or just things to kill. They would massacre them all and make sport out of it.

"Full speed ahead," said the Captain. "Be ready to drop cargo."

♦

Jotunn Daughter

Kharla watched as a trio of hunters left the settlement. Their lumbering mounts, titanic camels with twin shaggy humps, vanishing into the distant steppe. Three more young Jotunn men to bring back food, fur and ivory.

She hoped Ivann would bring her something. She'd marry him if he asked.

Kharla stood in the doorway of her mother's Dive. Her hard square face had an Amazonian beauty that was desired amongst Jotunn men. Her kinked black hair hung halfway down her back. The deep throated Rus-Hyborean rap rolled over the radio behind her. Her brother cooking in the back always played it.

Two elders sat by the window playing a card game. Their faces were dark and wrinkled like boiled leather and hair like pale ropes. They enjoyed their game quietly.

Kharla returned to her tasks. She crushed onions with the side of a cleaver, ground dried fish into powder, boiled megafauna bones into stock and seared flanks of elk meat. The dive was always a place for everyone. The lunch rush would hit be hitting soon.

The Rus-Hyborean rap continued to boom from the stereo.

Kharla preferred the operatic Europa metal.

The door chimed open as Kharla dropped bundles of buckwheat noodles into the boiling water. Sweat dripped down her face.

Kharla wiped her hands and stepped out into the dining area. "Welcome to-"

She froze.

In the doorway stood a silhouette. Someone barely standing halfway up the height of the doorway. Barely child-sized if they weren't so thin. Jotunn children were notoriously big boned little monsters.

The customer stepped inside, a bag over her shoulder. Her blue eyes were like tiny sparking beads. She climbed into a table like it was a ladder.

"Greetings," she said in half-decent VolgaJotunn.

The human sat like an awkward child in a chair, waiting for Kharla to overcome her shock. *Humans never come this far north.*

♦

Passage

"Where are we even headed?" asked Brother Bec as he rubbed his hands together, trying to keep warm.

"Just need to see our heading!" barked Conrad, the captain of this insane venture. Their new search for the Northwest Passage had been a brutal battle against both the elements and themselves.

Now the Captain and Brother Bec, the missionary on this mission, were in a small dingy checking their next heading. It was early, much of the crew was still asleep. Loyal officers remained on deck.

Day was perpetual in this realm of ice and water, however.

Their galley sat a few hundred yards back, waiting in a bay between two huge mountainous icebergs.

Brother Bec blew into his shivering gloves.

They searched through the next few streams of perfectly black water. The Captain scaled a huge and dangerous mound of ice until he saw the next route. He cackled with triumph and slid back into the boat. The dingy rocked, the monk grimaced at the Captain's adventurous frivolity.

Bec turned back at the sound of a ringing bell.

"No!" hissed Conrad.

They rushed back towards the rowboat, paddling furiously. When they turned a corner back into the bay, the ship was gone.

"Those… Those Traitors!" roared the Captain.

Bec had been sure of the loyalty of the remaining officers.

Conrad's popularity amongst the crew had run low, but not this low. That's what Bec thought, then he looked down.

"Lord protect us."

Conrad's roaring died.

Below the boat, in the deep black water was the huge face of a woman. At least fifty-feet across with glistening green skin and black speckles down her cheeks. A huge smile grew across her face with thousands of jagged teeth. Her hair, like tentacles, reached up through the surface of the water.

The men screamed.

◆

Koi

The fat multi-coloured fish lazed around in their pools. Flubbing lips producing bubbles. The garden filled with pools, bridges and arching trees. A beautiful glade that played host to a battle.

Two magicians of bastardized skill whipped spells at one another with reckless abandon.

Water rustled from the fountains. Feet clattered against wooden boards. A witch with a wand threw a ball of light at her opponent. The warlock parried away the attacks with a skull-tipped staff.

"Why'd you do it!?" hissed the warlock. "We were supposed to do this together!"

"I'm not waiting around for you anymore!" she fired another string of burning spells. A cluster of energies spiraled and dived towards him.

He clacked the staff against the wooden bridge. A stream of water flew into the air and spiraled out into a shield.

Steam hissed and swallowed the attacks.

Both mages were exhausted. Their magic instruments cracked and burned with use. Magic needed a source. Wands and staffs provided the fuel for many spells. When those ran out, the magic would eat the casters. Their hands and arms already covered in flecks of pale MagesBlyte.

The witch rushed forward with more reckless spells.

The koi watched, an unimpressed audience for a battle with years of tension built into it. All they could see was two young humans with the power of gods having a spat.

♦

Crashing

The orc, Brik, landed hard on the next level of rock. His knees groaned. Around him water crashed. His trousers with soaked. He had gone shirtless. His grey-green chest heaved from the battle.

In his burly hand, a four-foot long curved blade with an extended handle. A strange weapon for an orc. His brother's blade.

His dead brother's blade.

Roars echoed over the thundering waterfall. Another orc,

this one taller and leaner than Brik, with emerald green skin. It carried a cleaverblade with blinding speed.

They slammed into each other. Heavy blades biting into one another. Water rolled off their broad backs. They roared with yellow fangs and iron-hard muscle bulged beneath their hides.

Brik slid back on bare feet. This was a pure fight. Just them and their chosen blades. The tall one *did* have the advantage in the chaotic conditions, attacking from above.

Brik rolled and tumbled off the rocky plateau. The waterfall was flanked with shelves of rock all the way down the cliff side. Greenery hung around the falls, swaying in the daylight.

Brik crashed through the pillar of churning white water. He landed hard again. His emerald opponent at his heels.

Brik caught the cleaveblade and let it slide off the curve of his sword. He dug into his opponent's guard, slamming the hilt into the orc's throat. It croaked and retreated through the water.

They battled from rocky outcrop to rocky outcrop. Dashing and attacking through the waterfall. The sun blazed high above, sending rainbow colours across their green skin in the shadow of the plateaus. Metal blows clanged across the valley below.

They went back and forth between attacking and retreating, taking turns as metal vibrated their arms and exhaustion tugged at their legs.

Brik's opponent was as skilled as he was strong. They were equals until one would finally tire or make a mistake.

They slammed into each other, losing footing. They both fell over and were sent plummeting down the waterfall. The refracted light glinted with green. They crashed into the low pool, mid-way up the waterfall.

There was still a long way down.

The pair gathered themselves up at the edge of the pool, just where the water rushed over the side. Bursting like jets around scattered rocks. They rose in knee deep water and the battle resumed.

♦

Short-Faced Bear

Jhonas crawled on his stomach, reducing his profile. He moved slowly and downwind from the den. Snow soaked his fur lined wool tunic. His massive frame shivered from the long days of intense cold.

He halted at the edge of the tree line. The conifers provided what little cover they could for a Jotunn.

Jhonas took his scope from his belt and peered through the lens.

In the distance, he perceived a crag of rock amongst the forests. The distant Ural Mountains were a faint blue saw blade along the horizon. The young Jotunn had never been this far west since his father took him on a business trip to the capital. That was almost twenty-years ago. Jhonas had more immediate concerns.

He zeroed in on a shadowed section of rock. A natural shelter.

Jhonas licked his lips.

Before long, a huge lumbering bear stepped into the dimming afternoon light. It stood almost seven-feet at the shoulders. It could stand well past Jhonas's eight feet on its hind legs.

It sat and licked its paw. Claws like metal shears. Bristly grey fur and a squashed pale face.

It had been raiding nearby sheep and elk flocks. A human died defending his flocks. *Damn little fools.*

The bones scattered around the den told Jhonas he had found the right bear.

He took his cannon of his back and loaded the shell. To a human the shell would be a 20 Gauge slug. The brass was warm in his hand. He loaded it and pushed the bolt forward until he felt the satisfying click.

He began crawling towards his target. It was a shame that the bear needed to die.

♦

Giant Trail

Sixteen Jotunns traveled in a line through a dense winter forest. The bare winter trees went on seemingly forever.

Chieftain Akat's heavy black eyes surveyed from left to right. His immense mass filled the pathway, his already huge shoulders bulked up from his mammoth hide cloak.

He followed at the second-last spot in the line, as all Chieftain's should.

Only here can I see all that goes on. His wife, Kata, was immediately in front of him. The rest of the Clan lumbered forward. The Elders and children disbursed throughout. He kept a watchful eye on them.

His back was watched by his younger brother, Rame.

Both carried long-barreled cannons on the shoulders and pick-axes on their belts.

"I don't like this place," said Rame. "We're vulnerable. Only the children could get through those trees."

The implication was clear. If they were ambushed, especially if by humans, they would be vulnerable and almost unable to move. The foliage was too dense for a Jotunn to move effectively.

Humans, like vermin, could attack and vanish.

Akat thought of the children. He agreed with his brother and leaned to Kata to double the Clan's pace. The children would complain, Elder Almon would struggle, but they needed to move.

The line hurried. They didn't panic. They trusted their Chieftain. Their gigantic feet booming through the forest. Jotunns were strong, they would make it.

The path swerved left and right, before halting. Freshly chopped logs piled into a rudimentary palisade blocked the trail.

Akat drew his cannon. His shark-like eyes searching.

Something snapped.

♦

Arrival

"Holy shit," said Craz on the deck of the ship. It had taken the Goblin four months to reach his destination from the Underground.

First an airship from the 9th District to Franco, then a charter bus to NeoAnglia, then a vessel to the Carib Republics, before finally charting a ship to West Africa. It had been a long and interesting trip; full of fascinating people, new foods and beautiful sights. All of it paled compared to now.

He had watched the feeds and vids. He had met many from the African Kingdoms visiting the Underground. He had even talked to Exposed persons who reported the continent was nothing but war, poverty and AIDS.

Damn ignorant fools.

On the deck of the ship, Craz stood in awe of the great city that spread out before him.

The ports were organized chaos of tankers and galleys bringing in goods and people from all over the world. Cranes like serpents lifted steel crates into warehouse yards. People by the thousands arrived on ships. Many of them black-skinned humans wearing brilliant colourful dresses and shirts, like swaying flowers. Many others were Jackal or Eagle-headed Coptics, spotted hunched lycanthropes and other strange humanoids and wondrous Sapients.

Beyond the port, the skyline grew like a forest of glass and gold spires. Gleaming in the bright sunny day like a dragon's horde. Airships hovered like lazy silver beetles. Hovercrafts, which *did* originate from the Underground but had clearly been perfected here, zipped around like sparkling diamond flies.

He rushed to the rail and saw a boardwalk full of people. Shops of a thousand different colours and smells, fabrics and rugs of a million different shades. It was like Craz's entire world had gone from black-and-white to full technicolour.

He gasped. A zebra-drawn chariot carried a local aristocrat through boardwalk. People scattered out of his way. His bare black chest glittered with gold necklaces. In one corner, an immense golden gorilla, easily the size of a Jotunn, sat doing tricks for gaggles of human children.

Craz was in complete awe. It was like the Underground had been spilled out into the sun and bloomed into a rainbow garden.

♦

Spear

Branches crashed, trees snapped, a deep yell cut through the trumpeting chaos of the forest. The young Jotunn hunter, Jhonas, was thrown against a conifer. The tree snapped like a child tumbling into a sapling.

He groaned on the snow-covered ground. His shoulder bled from a deep wound. His fur-lined tunic was torn. His face was covered in blood and dark hair a tangled mess. He looked up with his black eyes just as thundering crashes hurtled in his direction.

He had lost his cannon in the failed attack.

Jhonas climbed to his feet. Eight feet of Siberian Jotunn. He was battered, but never beaten.

The trumpeting calls grew closer. Birds scattered from the forest.

Jhonas considered drawing his pick-axe and dagger, but he saw a broken tree trunk a few yards away. Straight and strong enough to hold effectively with a jagged point.

From between a pair of snow swept conifers charged the attacking beast. A Gompho.

Half the size of a mammoth, therefore bigger than a bull rhino, it charged towards Jhonas. Squat burly body covered in bristly brown fur. From its upper and lower jaws grew short pointed tusks. A four-pronged charge of interlocking ivory, with a short flexible trunk.

Its stampede shook the ground. Snow fell from trees.

Jhonas jumped for the rudimentary spear. He gripped it with white-knuckled desperation to survive and braced it against the ground, point out.

An unintelligible roar slipped from his lips.

♦

Observation

The Observation Craft, IRV Forunta, had been searching the South Pacific for three weeks. Madison Warwich scanned the expanse of water with binoculars. A plain of emerald blue shimmering in all directions. Warwich hadn't seen her home of Dunwich in nearly a year.

She sat back down on a chair. Her silvery bionic leg creaked. It would need maintenance when they returned to port. The water-resistance finish wasn't as good as the box claimed.

"There's nothing out here," commented her second, a well-to-do Anglo named Bertram. An academic with decades of research, but only months field experience.

Warwich ignored him and continued searching the horizon. The sun beat overhead. Sweat beaded across their foreheads. The science vessel was comfortable and they had been well-provisioned. Tomorrow, however, they would have to return to an Andean port.

"It's a crying shame," said Bertram.

"Shut up."

"What?"

"Shut up!" she peered through her scope. "Look!"

In the distance was a small string of volcanic outcroppings. A craggy ripple of rock covered in sea plants and scurrying with crabs.

"It's an island," said Bertram.

"Is it now?"

The Science vessel moved closer to the island, but no matter how many knots they moved, the island remained some distance away.

"Ring the bell," said Warwich.

A master's student nodded and flicked a switch. From specialized speakers beneath the craft, a low rumbling song echoed through the water. A siren call for primordial titans.

Now the island moved towards them. Warwich leaned over the rail, grinning like an excited child. Her sunburnt arms were covered in kaiju and nautical tattoos. Her mane of unkempt brown curls pulled back.

The Leviathan swam past their ship. Over two hundred feet long with skin like igneous rock. A beaked face worn like bleached coral. Wide fins glided through the ocean. Schools of fish circled the titan. A floating ecosystem for a dozen unique species.

It was massive. Ancient. Almost a thousand years old. Maybe older if they could get samples.

Warwich peered through the water and saw its tiny black eyes. The eyes of an ancient sea god.

◆

Tundra

The Alaskan plains. Tundra. The Arctic Circle.

The frozen wasteland stretched in all directions. It reached the mountains to the south, the plains to the east and the ice fields in the north.

A trumpet boomed through the air.

A line of great mammoths, one of the last on the continent, marched onwards. Huge column legs covered in coarse brown fur. Trumpeting brays. The squeal of the calves. Their constant search for fodder drove them forward.

Their rumbling gate was enough to deter wolves and bears. The herd was too few now to be reliable prey for the monsters of the wastes. Those would search elsewhere sustenance.

That is, except for one.

A truck sat on a distant hill.

The poacher peered through his scope. He smiled, lowered the scope and watched with hungry anticipation.

He had hunted beasts from the forests of Rus, the mountains of AlphenHeim and the deserts of the Mali Empire. He feared no government, no beast and no monster. *The enviromentalists can try and stop me. The Goblin Clans can try to stop me.* None could.

He whispered over the radio. "Boys, we have ourselves a hunt tonight. Be impressive to say we slayed the last of the American Mammoths."

The vilest predator thought nothing of feeding, only of sport, the thrill of the hunt.

The poacher was that kind of predator.

◆

Shore

"She isn't going to marry you," said Sebastian.

105

"You don't know that," said Carlos. "It's been a long time coming and she knows it."

The pair walked down a pristine white beach. They patrolled for pirates and landing parties, anyone coming shore. They were foot soldiers for Esteban de la Cruz, a lord on the Mexica coast. The palm trees swayed in the breeze. The sky was growing dark.

"I'm just saying," said Sebastian. "Prepare for disappointment."

"Fuck you…"

Their boots crunched against debris. Carlos stopped. A wooden plank stuck in the sand. Carlos kneeled, finding a piece of rope. Sebastian grimaced, poking at more debris with his rifle. Their eyes met and the conclusion was simple. There had been a shipwreck.

Sebastian followed marks from the water towards the trees. A collection of footprints leading into the coastal jungle.

"Call it in," said Sebastian. Lord Cruz and his guard would have quite a sporting time hunting down trespassers in the jungles.

Carlos wasn't listening. He was looking out towards the sea. The waves lapped against the shore. The sky was darkening, a storm was coming in.

Both men froze.

A ripple in the distance grew into a shadow. A huge figure waded into the shallows and towards the shore. A titanic monster of terrible might. A prehistoric god from the depths, a curse on the coast of Mexica.

The men bolted, fleeing desperately back towards the fortress-city.

Whatever had caused the shipwreck was coming to raid the coast as well.

♦

Whale Eater

It was the last of the Atlantic Skyeaters. Chalk grey hide worn and rock-like, blasted by the winds and water. Its body eroded like the jagged Fist of Ymir. Black horns sprouted a crown over its head, black spikes down its back and along its jaws. Its monstrous head would have rivaled most bull theropods.

Vivid crystal eyes swept the ocean.

From the research vessel, the expedition team watched. Madison Warwich was completely enraptured by the beast.

Its wings could wrap themselves around the vessel.

"What is that? Eighty feet wingspan?" asked Madison to Diego.

He blinked. "Over a hundred."

It glided over the ocean with a godly elegance. Its immense size help up by arctic winds, lighter than air biology and specialized bone structure. Diego could have gone on for hours about the dragon's anatomy, but they were too awed by the creature.

It angled itself just over the surface of the water. The buzzing hordes of sea birds and pygmy Silverwing dragons split and scattered, like opening curtains to the main act.

Isik, in the local Inuktitut, meaning smoke. The great dragon flew motionless, like a hovering statue, water spraying behind from the jetstream left by its titanic size.

The dragon dragged its clawed talons through the water. White foam exploded. Its sword-sized talons vanished into the black waters. A moment of pure silence followed. Madison clutched the rail of the ship. She was sweating within her parka. Her voice caught in her throat. The only sound was the constant roar of the ocean.

Water exploded. A geyser of foam erupted at the dragon's ankles. It angled its wings, carrying itself higher through the air.

In its talons, a beluga whale calf. The poor animal had come to the surface to breathe and lingered too long. Black ivory punctured the off-white flesh. Ribbons of hot mammal blood dripped through the air.

"Brace!" shouted Captain Nank.

The dragon flew past the nose of the ship, unbothered by the unnatural presence. The herculean winds slammed into Madison, she almost lost her balance on her bionic leg. She redoubled her grip on the railing. Icy ocean spray flecked her face.

Isik flapped his titanic wings, thunderclaps echoed. The birds and pygmy dragons squawked in their thousands as they returned to their feeding on the clouds of fish below the black water.

Isik flew up and over the distant shoreline of cliffs. Up and out of sight.

The last of his species. The subject of the team of researchers and documentarians. None had any idea a band of poachers were already in the territory. Their only aim to slay the last of the great arctic dragons.

◆

Mountain Guest

The temples grew around the mountain pools. Streams from the high Himalayan peaks brought the coldest clearest water through the valley. The pools shimmered in the sunlight of the clear day.

The young monk, Lei Fan, got up from his perch at the base of the tower. The mountain air bit at his cheeks. His red and saffron robes billowed in the winds. In his hands he clutched a dime novel from the lowlands. He had no possessions, but the abbot, always the radical, encouraged taking joy in simple things.

The temple gong echoed.

Lei Fan continued reading, enjoying the simple escapism by some distant American author.

The gong echoed three more times. *Someone had arrived.*

He rushed down the trail between the needle-covered trees. His beaded necklace clattered against his chest. His slippers slapped against the step stones.

When he arrived at the temple-complex, activity could be seen with monks rushing towards the gates. An immense structure of galleries, shrines and chambers with sloped tiled roofs. Lei Fan rushed through the gates and into the courtyard.

From the entrance, one could see the main temple and the shrine to the Buddha. The holy visage of the calm golden titan, his hands held in perfect form. Trails of incense like grey ribbons floating past the Holy Buddha's face.

In the courtyard, the Abbot stood with the visitor.

A nine-foot-tall giant had arrived. Wrapped in a grey velvet tunic lined with fur. A face as rugged as the mountainside with eyes as clear blue as water.

The Jotunn from the far north, beyond the steppe and valleys. He leaned on a curved bladed spear, the haft the size of a tree. His fists of marbled blue-grey and tanned skin.

Lei Fan gulped, slid the book into his robes and hurried to join the welcoming party. As was expected.

They bowed to the Jotunn, offered their blessings and services.

What is a Jotunn doing here? They never came this far south.

♦

PART 5
THE WAR

"2035 by Gregorian, what grew out of the unification of the Yarl-doms was a war unparalleled in its reach and destruction."

Marquis

Marquis Garnell examined the map on his table. West of Franco was the backwater Yarldoms. A collection of feudal gang-led towns and skraelbands.

Disgusting.

Garnell paced around his office. As the most western vassalage of Franco, he had many associations with the Yarldoms. Some of the Eastern-most Yarls were amiable and civilized. Particularly Mistress Kenta.

She had died, many of them had.

Civil strife had driven the already divided region into warring factions. Before the violence could escalate beyond a few skirmishes and raids and into the first total war of the region, a marriage had produced a single unified country.

A single unified nation had appeared on the Marquis's western border.

A single nation where gangsters, lordlings, and mobs of primitives had existed.

Garnell had yet to receive his orders from the Capital.

He paced around the office more nervously.

What can we even do?

Reports said the new King of the Yarldoms, the son of Isumi Kenta, was a confirmed necromancer.

Filth. Now they play at ruling a divided nation.

His queen was a seventeen-year-old girl. The sister of one of the would-be-warlords.

A land ruled by a child and a warlock. A land filled with ravaging barbarian Eastlanders and savage Skraelings. A land with Necromancers and Knights and old deep magic of the First Peoples.

Perhaps he was giving the new King and Queen too much credit. Divisions in the Yarldoms were old and very well entrenched. The Skraelings were chomping at a chance to dethrone the Eastlanders. The Eastlander's lost their greatest advocate. Yarls dropping left and right. Everyone in between were unsure of who to back.

It would all play out in due time. Uncertainty was the companion to power. The mighty Sword of Damocles.

But the Marquis had to admit, this was the first time in a long time he felt fear.

♦

Timber

Francis rubbed his hands over the fire, trying to work warmth back into his fingers. The campfire crackled and sent sparks up into the starlit sky.

The other two lumberjacks huddled close to the fire. Leo and Kalvin. *Good Franco boys.*

Their beards were flecked with ice. They were too cold and too tired to get up and just go to bed in their tents. *It was a mistake to stay out for this much of the winter.* They had been sending logs down the river throughout the fall and when the position to stay and keep the site safe came, they jumped at the offer for double pay.

"Too fucking cold," said Leo.

Kalvin scoffed. "You say that every ten minutes. Just shut your trap."

"Fuck you."

"Enough," said Francis. "I've decided; fuck the company. We'll head back to town in the morning."

They both nodded.

"Find some good ladies," said Francis with a smirk. "Keep our sides warm."

The men laughed.

Leo looked up. His curled blonde moustache hung with icicles. "I heard the nobility may go to war."

"They always go to war."

"Not with each other!" said Leo. "To the west. With the Yarldoms. Or the Goblins."

A twig snapped.

Francis ignored the question. He didn't have an answer. He stood up, bolt-action rifle in hand. His hatchet was lodged in the stump next to him.

The men were silent.

Francis scanned his surroundings.

In the dark surrounded the worksite was nothing but howling with and drifting snow. He narrowed his eyes. A pair of eyes starred back. They reflected the light like tiny moons.

♦

Herdsmen

"War is coming," said Maxi.

"It's not our problem," said his father, Ghengr. Both rode atop their titanic mounts. Ghengr rode his sweetheart, Moira. The lumbering beast reached up passed her head with her trunk, searching for treats in Ghengr's tunic. He laughed, teasing the shaggy pachyderm.

Maxi sighed. His father never understood. He was an old man and an old soul. Set in his ways, the old ways. Ghengr's winter dreadlocks hung around his huge shoulders.

Moira honked playfully.

"Dad, everything in the Feeds look worse day by day."

"You can't keep watching the world through screens," said Ghengr. "We have our lives here. Beyond problems of little people and short-lived fools."

The pair, atop their Mammoths, stood over a slope leading down into a shallow valley below. The grassy valley split by a river. A seemingly endless herd of Giant Elk shook the earth as it followed the river.

Beasts with bristling golden manes and wide branch-like antlers. They roamed freely in search of fresh pastures.

The Jotunn Herdsmen were merely guides and guardians. They pruned what could be spared.

"What happens when the Kheslat calls for a draft?"

Ghengr laughed. "Son, the wars you're talking about are on the other side the world…"

"Dad," said Maxi, looking at his father. They looked a world apart. Maxi took after his mother's Hyborean blonde hair and icy eyes, where Ghengr was a proper Siberian Jotunn with dark tanned skin. Maxi pointed directly north. "When north becomes south, those feuding kingdoms are only a few thousand miles away. The ice is melting. The world is changing. The herds are growing smaller and moving farther north."

Ghengr had stopped laughing.

Maxi kicked his mount, Hope, into a lumbering trot. "Dad, Hyperborea has a new destiny and my generation will have to learn to survive it."

Ghengr sighed and followed. "I know son. I just wish it wasn't so."

"We don't get to choose our destiny."

"Now you sound like your mother…"

♦

Camouflage

A pair of fighters crouched in the underbrush flanking a waterfall. The foliage was dense and green. The humid smell of moss in the air. They hid in an inlet fifty feet above the river below. The road followed the river before turning north.

Reed knelt; her hand gripped a wet rock. Her dark brown face covered in crisscrossed camo paint.

"They coming?" asked Alga.

"Soon," said Reed, sniffing. "Let's get ready."

Alga was a burly Eastlander woman, like a bear with tits. Her red hair matted with clay and mud.

Both women were invisible to wandering eyes.

Both were volunteers for the new Royal Army. Both swore oaths to King and Country. A new and alien concept to both of them.

Reed was OjiCree. She had left her band when her step-brother got handsy and her family did nothing. *Asshole must be dead by now.*

Now two women from previously warring peoples were hunting down new invaders and traitors.

They set up their position. The noise of the waterfall was the perfect disguise. They pulled leaves and foliage to further hide their position. The noise would hide the eventual gunshot.

Alga passed Reed a canteen. Reed nodded thanks.

"You think we can win?" whispered Alga.

The Yarldoms were a single country now. That attracted enemies, vultures, and foreign invasion. The new government was working with band leaders and chiefs to get the OjiCree the resources they needed.

After a moment's pause, Reed sighed. "No. I don't think so… but I'd rather be on the losing side that stands for what's right. For all the things I could say about the King and Queen, they aren't the opposition."

Alga nodded. "Agreed. To Valhalla."

"Whatever," teased Reed.

A rumble echoed nearby. A long column of infantry approached along the road below. At their head, a Franco Marquis, riding in an open topped jeep with house flags.

Reed leaned into the sniper rifle and waited for Alga's go.

♦

Carapace

Tris sat in her arming chamber alone. The black metal walls rose up far too high than they needed to be. The fluorescent lights flickered. She rubbed her eyes with the calloused heels of her hands. Her burnished blonde hair fell in short bobs around her ears.

She wore little else besides black elastic undergarments. Her body was a living machine, nine feet tall, lithe, wiry and criss-crossed with hundreds of scars. She had spent thirty years in Jotunn Armed Forces. A Captain in the Special Forces now. A leader of black ops mission.

A Captain in the Queen's army. Army tattoos emblazoned on both shoulders. Those shoulders felt especially heavy. Tris had seen a lot in her career. More than most Jotunns. She looked up, the blue of her eyes almost covered the entire orb. Her Siberian cousins had eyes like a shark.

She stood up from the metal bench. The arming chamber was for officers to have some time to think as they prepared. It was dumb, but it was a tradition of sorts. The chamber was always painfully quiet.

On the wall, against a glowing pane of plastic, were her arms and armor.

The glossy black Carapace-6 Armor. Plates of unreflective black Skymetal, from the meteors that crashed down in the steppe and Siberia. The helmet, a blank mask of midnight chrome. A modern knight's harness. The bracers and greaves were like diamond plates, as deadly a weapon as her firearms and blades.

Tris touched the smooth breastplate. The metal was impossibly strong. Bullets and explosives shrugged off like annoying insects.

117

On either side; her weapons.

A heavy caliber firearm, like a submachine gun in shape, but firing .50 caliber bullets. Its box-like receiver and bullpup design was flexible at all rangers. In the field, they needed flexibility. They would be fighting armor and infantry, on open tundra and in cramped human cities.

Her sword, black Skymetal, was a heavy, diamond-like blade. Useful in the field. Tactical in its design. She touched the deep grooves in the metal.

She wished she could feel the breeze on her face, the smell of pine and feel a lover's hand on her hard cheek.

Not anymore, she thought. *Now is the time for war.*

She sat back down and called the armorers.

♦

Expanse

The sky seemed endless. Stretching far beyond anything imaginable for the young trooper. His slick black armor glistened in the grey light of the tundra. Everything was cold here.

Paal kneeled. The ground was cold and firm. Permafrost. He ran his gloved fingers through the scraggly grass. A tone blared in his ears. He looked up. The flickering symbols within his Battle-Mask told him the enemy was nearing.

Two miles away.

His brother stood next to him, carrying a Gauss Cannon like it was it was a rifle. *Big bastard.*

He was thankful his brother was with him.

More blips on the Heads-Up-Display warned Paal of the incoming army closing the distance.

Everything was so perfectly flat and endless out here. Like shallow waves of a pond, the occasional rise and dip in the tundra, but mostly endless frozen wasteland.

A few dozen yards behind Paal were the Titans.

Their huge stomping steps as the pilots lined up in a phalanx of steel and armor. They carried Gauss cannons the shape of pistols and pikes the size of telephone poles. VoidShields hovered around the formation like bubbles around a garden. Layers of projected armor against the enemy's poorer, but nonetheless deadly weaponry.

Paal stood up. The shakes started to course through his arms. He gripped his Lasrifle tightly to keep from shaking.

He glanced back at the formation of Titans. At its head was a single young woman. Dark-skinned with braids twisted into a bun. Her jade eyes narrowed and focused. Her left hand was a chrome bionic.

Paal had heard of her. A Pryomancer Aide of some Underground King.

The War had begun and Paal knew he had made a mistake to follow his brother into war.

His brother padded his shoulder. Paal couldn't see his face behind the BattleMask. Paal wanted to puke, he couldn't.

He couldn't let his brother down.

He couldn't let his brother see his doubts.

They would both die if he gave into fear.

Battlefield

Explosions rippled through the air. Popping like tumbling yellow candies across the sky. A beetle-shaped Battlecraft exploded and tumbled down through the sky before lodging itself into a hillside.

The battlefield stretched as far as the eye could see. Flashes of light, screams and the crash of metal.

What began as a scouting skirmish where two forces of outriders on dirt bikes literally stumbled into each other, had escalated when infantry, air support and Titan phalanxes were called in.

Captain Tina Bolton hugged the edge of a sloping hill. *There's no cover on this godforsaken tundra.*

Behind her were twenty jacketed soldiers with lasrifles. A mix of mostly Eastlanders, Anglos and Francos, a genuine mix of Alliance forces.

Her second, Lieutenant Jem Black Leaf, an OjiCree, crouched next to her. Jem carried an assault rifle with a launcher.

Bolton circled the edge of an outcropping.

Across a plateau, stomped a huge Heavy-Artillery Titan. It's red and chrome armor blasted with dust and dirt. It raised its fist and fired a thundering stream of heavy calibre gunfire. The ground shook. On its shoulder sat a glowing blue Gauss Canon.

Orders: Destroy.

Bolton kneeled next to Black Leaf. "Take your half and go around the back. We'll come from the flank. You attack in two minutes."

They synced timers. Jem nodded. "Don't get killed."

"Same to you."

Jem pumped her fist and her anti-armor platoon followed. Bolton waved her soldiers to spread out and wait for Jem to launch the rear attack.

More explosions rippled through the sky. The main clash a klick away had become a literal maelstrom as magicians, titans, technopaths and demigods slugged it out. Shattering the permafrost like glass, creating mountains and death out of the wasteland.

Bolton watched the time elapse.

But Black Leaf's anti-armor didn't strike.

Bolton licked her lips. *I'm about to get my men killed.* They had to destroy the Titan, or more would die. She aimed her lasrifle at the Titan's cockpit and fired.

◆

War Machine

This was a mistake, thought Baron Cadre. *This entire mission was a mistake.*

Franco had entered the war with the belief that their own versions of the so called NewTech, was superior to their enemies'. They had skipped the trial-and-error phase and could build the most advanced models.

Their weapons were beautifully made, powerful, maybe even elegant. They were works of art and war.

He threw the controls forward, the Colossus stepped forward into an aggressive stance. His twenty-five-foot-tall Colossus appeared like an elegant suit of shining gothic armor. The proportions were a bit off and it lacked a head, but it was a fluid and powerful machine. Silver plating and fluted panels was stark against the dark mountain pass.

Mist swirled around the titan's legs.

He adjusted the whirling gyros which kept the Colossus balanced. He re-gripped the controls, the titan's vambraces gripped its sword with both hands.

An elegant sabre of high tensile Damascus steel. Reinforced with fullers and welded bars.

The rugged survivability of the enemy's Colossi were too much.

Franco put its ego above practicality.

Around Cadre's Colossus were the broken pieces of another machine. Its clumsy toy-robot proportions shattered. The pilot dead within the cracked cockpit.

It had damaged Cadre's comm system and his wrist-mounted gauss cannon. Leaving him only the sword. The warning siren blared at incoming threats. He already knew they were coming.

Baron Cadre prayed to the Christ God as five other rugged machines with black and red armor charged up the passed. Machineguns firing on their shoulders.

Gunfire sparked off the Baron's titan. He grit his teeth and charged.

♦

Mirror Water

It was too early in the season for the fountains or for the dead plants to be cleaned out. The gardens remained as empty and dead as a mausoleum. The crisp rainy chill of spring was welcomed, but summer awaited.

The promising cherry blossoms grinned with lush vibrancy around the pool. The water as clear and smooth as a mirror, reflecting its surroundings.

Metal clashed.

The two combatants bounced off the mirror water. Lighter beyond possibility. They floated across the water, each step sent ripples across the glassy water. They landed with perfect elegance back on the stone pathways.

They glared at each other, once so intimate, now they had no other choice.

One, with pointed-ears and wearing flowing black silks from head to toe. Nothing but a strip of copper-coloured flesh exposed and a pair of vivid violet eyes. In her white gloved hands she held a long straight-bladed sword with a gold tassel on the hilt.

Her opponent, also with pointed ears wore rough leather and denim. Her ebony dark face held in a pained grimace. In a silvery bionic hand she held another straight-bladed sword with a brass hilt. Her jade eyes intense.

They leapt back into action, two graceful immortals gliding across the water. Metal clanged over the pool.

The breeze sent spirals of cherry pedals dancing around the two figures.

A duel of eternal intensity between two former lovers.

They had chosen opposing sides of the war.

♦

CANAL

There wasn't a soul along the boardwalk. It was silent.

Well, that wasn't entirely true. He could hear the city across the water. The blare of barges and galleys, traffic and sirens. An endless metropolis with millions of individual lives; equal parts tragedy and comedy. All a distant idea. They weren't even real. There was the excited chirps and songs of spring time. The greenish blue canal swam by casually, rippling as the trees rustled.

It was a perfect picture as could be imagined. He sat in quiet contemplation.

Not a soul to spoil his clear mind and perfect image.

"A perfect place to die," he admitted to himself.

He could not find a better picture. Life would forever pale in comparison. Pain, heartbreak, loss.

And that guardrail was so low.

He wondered what would happen.

Someone would find his bag abandoned on the bench. His wallet, phone, passport. He would be identified quickly, assuming they found the body at all.

His family would be notified halfway across the country, might as well be a different planet.

"He was on vacation…" they would say, confused, angry, destroyed.

They would mourn and be missing a chunk of their lives forever. No matter what his brain told him otherwise, he knew that was true.

He would never find a better time in his life. Alone, quiet and peaceful.

He exhaled, gathered his bag and carried on with his walk. *That* was one version of the story that wouldn't happen.

He no longer and for the first time in forever, did not feel the need. He felt the weight leave his chest for the first time.

For the first time he believed the words.

"It's going to be okay."

◆

AFTERWORD

How do you become a writer? You write. Pretty easy answer, right?

Anyone who has ever sat down to write or fought to find the time or tried to find the motivation to write when the time opens up knows how hard it can be.

In 2019, when I was struggling through depression, unemployment and anxiety, I made one rule for myself. Publish content every week for a year. Every week I posted a one-page flash fiction for an entire year. I ended up with nearly a hundred small pieces. Around seventy ended up on my website.

All of them were glimpses of a fantasy world I was learning how to build and how to write. Exploring feelings, characters, tone, mystery and horror in all its forms. I rarely wrote a story with a plot twist or character beat in mind. It was always on mood, imagery, emotion, and motion. I would sit in forests, gardens, shopping malls, city squares and even churches and come up with moments of action, mystery, and terror.

Through these pieces I slowly got some feedback and encouragement. I learned through trial and error what people respond most strongly too and how to twist the knife when I wanted to. So here they all are. In a single place.

On the Wrong Side. Nothing is right anymore.

These are The Veiled Sagas.

Z. F. Sigurdson

◆